Table of Contents

OJIBWE GIIZHIG ANUNG MASINAAIGAN

Ojibwe Sky Star Map

ZIIGWAN ~ Spring

Mishi Bizhiw, Great Panther; *Gaadidnaway*, Curly Tail

Madoodiswan, Sweat Lodge

Ikwe'anung, Women's Star, Venus

Waabun'anung, Morning Star

Ningobi'anung, Evening Star

Giizis, Sun

NIIBIN ~ Summer

Ajijaak/Bineshi Okanin, Crane/Skeleton Bird

Noondeshin Bemaadizid, Exhausted Bather

Nanaboujou, Nanaboujou

Dibik-giizis, Night Sun, Moon

Ishpeming, Sky Above, Universe

THE WOLF'S TRAIL

AN OJIBWE STORY, TOLD BY WOLVES

A NOVEL BY

THOMAS D. PEACOCK

Holy Cow! Press
Duluth, Minnesota
2020

Cover painting, "Eternity," by James O'Connell.
"Ojibwe Giizhig Anung Masinaagin—Ojibwe Sky Star Map," a Native Skywatchers star map,
created by A. Lee, W. Wilson, C. Gawboy, © 2012 and reprinted by permission.
Versions of the chapters *The Arrival* and *The Boy* were previously published
in *The Tao of Nookomis* (2020), second edition.
Wolf map created by Patrick Rolo.
Author photograph by Betsy Albert-Peacock.
Book and cover design by Anton Khodakovsky.

Printed and bound in the United States of America.
First printing, Spring, 2020
ISBN 978-15136456-2-9
10 9 8 7 6 5

ACKNOWLEDGEMENTS

The Wolf's Trail would not have been possible without the advice and expertise from many others. Mike Schrage, Wildlife Biologist for the Fond du Lac Band of Lake Superior Ojibwe provided me with invaluable knowledge of wolf social behavior. He took time to read the rough manuscript and offered his expertise as one who has an immense storehouse of wolf knowledge. Terry Gibson (Bayfield and Madison, WI) also played an important editing role, offering his editing expertise as an avid reader. Felicia Schneiderhan was an extraordinary editor, an expert in structure and organization, spelling, grammar, punctuation and content. Demaris Britton of Apostle Islands Booksellers read and edited one of the initial drafts of the story and gave me important encouragement to move the story forward, telling me that it was worth the telling. My wife Betsy, always my most valuable editor, who has read draft after draft of each chapter and shared ideas all along the way. I'm also indebted to the Minnesota State Arts Board, who awarded me an individual artists grant to develop the manuscript. And finally, an acknowledgement to Jim Perlman, publisher, who has a keen eye for a story worth sharing, and found this one compelling enough to put in a book. To each of them I am deeply indebted.

Holy Cow! Press projects are funded in part by grant awards from the Ben and Jeanne Overman Charitable Trust, the Elmer L. and Eleanor J. Andersen Foundation, the Lenfestey Family Foundation, Schwegman Lundberg & Woessner, P.A., and by gifts from generous individual donors. We are grateful to Springboard for the Arts for their support as our fiscal sponsor.

Holy Cow! Press books are distributed to the trade by Consortium Book Sales & Distribution, c/o Ingram Publisher Services, Inc., 210 American Drive, Jackson, TN 38301.

For inquiries, please write to: HOLY COW! PRESS,
Post Office Box 3170, Mount Royal Station, Duluth, MN 55803.
Visit *www.holycowpress.org*

To my grandparents,

Harry and Emma (Bandle) Morrissette,

Michael Peacock and Marie (Bear) Diver,

and the wolves of *Nagahchiwanong* and *Miskwabekong*

DAGWAAGIN ~ Fall

Mooz, Moose

Bugonagiizhig, Hole in the Sky, Pleiades

Madoo'asinik, Sweating Stones, Pleiades

Waawaate, Aurora Borealis, Northern Lights

Jiibayag niimi'idiway, Spirits Dancing, Aurora Borealis

Gaagige Giizhig, Forever Sky, Universe

GIWEDINANG ~ North

Maang, Loon   *Giwedin'anung*, North Star, Polaris   *Ojiig*, Fisher

BIBOON ~ Winter

Biboonkeonini, Wintermaker

Maingan Mikan, Wolf Trail, Ecliptic

Jiibaykona, Spirit Path, Milky Way

Jiibay Ziibi, River of Souls, Milky Way

Gwiingwa, Shooting star, Meteor

Anung Nibwakawin, Star Wisdom

Dagwaac Fall

Biboon Winter

Original Painting by Annette S. Lee & William P. Wilson, © 2012; Ojibwe Language Consultant: William Wilson

Map Created By Annette S. Lee, William Wilson, Carl Gawboy © 2012

Additional Reference: C. Gawboy, W. Wilson, M. Price, T. Kinew

Annette S Lee et William...

MISKWABEKONG

SPIRIT
ISLAND

ECHO VALLEY
WOLF PACK

NAGACHIWANONG

PIPESTONE INDIAN SCHOOL

PREFACE

MAYBE YOU ARE OUT WALKING on a trail and see the footprints of a wolf in the mud, the tracks a day or two old, or fresh, imprints large or small, or nearly washed away by rain, or partially covered by fallen leaves. Each possibility has a story about a wolf that happened upon the trail the day before, or a moment ago, of it tracking a rabbit or hunting mice or voles, or following the scent of a deer. And that moment of finding the tracks contains a part of the whole of the wolf's story. Of when it was just a pup, born into a pack that lives somewhere in the vicinity of the trail, of roughhousing with its sisters and brothers and cousins, learning to hunt, becoming the alpha female or male or being the beta, mid-level wolf, or omega, leading, losing its role as alpha with age and the arrival of another who was bigger, stronger, smarter, or always being a mid-level wolf, or omega, the submissive one. And then, one day, yesterday, the day before, today, a moment ago, it came upon and followed a trail, and on that day in that season you also happened upon the same trail. And the moment you came upon what you came upon, a footprint, a wolf, you entered the story – the wolf, you.

That is how this story was born.

Out of nothing he made rock, water, fire, and wind. Into each he breathed the breath of life. On each he bestowed with his breath a different essence and nature. Each substance had its own power, which became its soul-spirit.

From these four substances Kitche Manitou (Creator) created the physical world of sun, stars, moon, and earth.

—Johnston, B. (1976). *Ojibway Heritage*.
Lincoln, Nebraska: University of Nebraska Press

CHAPTER I

The Naming of Aki

(Wisdom, Truth)

I AM OF THE WOLVES FROM the hills that overlook the river that flows through Nagahchiwanong, the bottom of the big lake, Gitchi Gumee, the one that bears the likeness of a wolf. This has been our home for so many generations we have long since lost count, since the times after the retreat of the last glacier, the one before that, and before that.

I'm old I suppose, nine winters, certainly old for a wolf. I first realized it when the pups began calling me *Zhi-shay'*, Uncle, and started asking me all kinds of questions because I supposedly possess knowledge, have wisdom. I don't know about that. *Zhi-shay'*, Uncle, they said, tell me about this. Uncle, tell me about that. At first I'd say I didn't know. Then they'd walk away and I'd hear them whispering. He knows, he does. Or he doesn't know. Maybe we should ask another uncle who knows something. Maybe this uncle is dumb. Most of the time though, I'd say, later. Tonight, tomorrow night, after I have gotten approval through *Giniw*, Golden Eagle, the beta male, and then *Ogema*, Leader, the alpha male, after the hunt, after this, after that, we'll gather in circle.

We'll talk story.

—

So I went to confer with *Giniw* first.

"I want to talk story with the pups, they've been asking."

He gave me that look, begrudging, that's his job, and took me over to *Ogema*.

Neither is much for words.

The alpha said, "Tell them everything."

So that's what I've done.

I wasn't sure where to even begin. I mean, I could go on and on with stories forever, if I was allowed to.

So I asked the pups.

"Where do you want me to begin?"

"*Zhi-shay'*," they said, "tell us about the humans. Start with them."

Even pups seem to possess an inherent understanding of the parallel relationship that exists between wolves and humans.

"What about us wolves?" I inquired back. I tease them like that sometimes. Most of them don't even know it is teasing. I continued.

"Maybe you could ask about us. We are, after all, wolves."

"But we heard you know all about the humans," my youngest, smallest nephew said, looking up at me. I call him Youngest Nephew because he was the last born in his litter and the smallest.

"We want you to tell us about them. Just in case."

"Just in case what?" I asked.

"Just in case we ever come upon them somewhere along the trail," said Youngest Nephew.

—

So several evenings later we gathered in circle and I told them the beginning story about wolves and humans, and in succeeding nights whenever I wasn't too tired from a hunt, or too full of meat or too hungry after too many days of unsuccessful hunts, or busy moving from camp to camp, or wanted to simply talk story, I'd continue on with the stories.

I thought it was important that I begin with the story of the creation, the Beginning. Young ones need to know the Creator's story of the universe and the place of wolves within the creation. Maybe someday when the pups are older and some of them become lost they will remember the teachings inside the story and it will help them find their way back onto the trail.

Here's the first one.

—

"Gather together," I began that night. "Ears in front. Tails behind.

"This is the story of the Beginning, when the Creator made everything from nothing, and when all was made, how it sent First Human and First Wolf, *Ma'iingan,* to walk *aki* (earth) and name all things. The story is what connects us to humans and explains the special relationship we both have with the Creator. So tonight I want you all to listen hard to me."

"Who is the Creator?" It was Youngest Nephew. He was a talented, albeit persistent questioner. He continued. "Is the Creator a wolf or human?"

"That's a good question," I replied. "I think the Creator is both, and everything else. I think the Creator is whatever it wants to be, whenever it wants to be. The Creator is the sky and air, winds, rain, and thunder. The Creator's essence, its perfect goodness, love, is in everything non-living and living, including us. When we do good things the Creator's love lives through us."

"I don't understand, Uncle," he continued his inquiry.

"I know," I replied. "I don't understand it all myself. I just know it is the truth."

"Will you tell us when you understand it all?"

"No, I'll keep it a secret and I won't tell anyone, ever," I replied. I was teasing, of course. I think he knew I was teasing because after I said it I nudged him with my snout and sent him rolling.

"Let me tell the story now," I said.

—

"This is the beginning story of wolves and humans told through the eyes of wolves. I suppose that is appropriate because both wolf and human are parallel beings whose ways have many similarities."

"What does that mean, similarities?" One of the pups interrupted when I used that word.

"It's the opposite of being not similar, but I really don't know," I said deadpan back at the lot of them. To be truthful, I'm not even sure what it means myself. Then I continued.

"What's similar?" I don't know who asked it, but it came from somewhere in the huddle of ears, snouts, fur, and tails.

"*Bizaan*. Quiet," I said. "Listen."

I need to say that often, it seems.

"So I'll begin with the story of the creation and naming of *aki*, earth. Even the humans would be able to recognize the story," I said, "as familiar, similar, different.

"This is the story as I have been told. Although there are other versions of the story among the various tribes of humans, the essential teachings remain the same, so we should use the lessons inside the story to live and treat one another. Among wolves this story has remained unchanged since the Beginning, when it was lived by *Ma'iingan,* the first Wolf, who, along with First Human, was given responsibility for naming *aki* (earth).

"In the Beginning there was nothing for a long, long time but the Creator. Then the Creator had a dream, a vision, about *aki* (earth) and all the planets, stars, and galaxies. In the dream, all things of the universe were made of rock, fire, water, and air. On *aki* (earth) and other selected worlds the Creator dreamed of living and non-living things.

"The dream went on the longest time.

"And when the Creator awoke, it made the dream real. Out of nothing the Creator made a burst of pure energy in the form of light, and from that came the four original substances – rock, fire, water, and air – and from these came everything in the Forever Sky, the universe. All of the stars and star clusters, all of the gaseous clouds and galaxies, all black holes, all voids in their complete blackness as well those places of both light and dark matter, all planets that circle all stars, all moons and comets and asteroids, dwarf planets and their moons. And on some worlds the Creator made life in so many forms they would be unrecognizable in other worlds, and yet each was made to represent the Creator's unique expression of itself. And to all life the Creator breathed some of its very essence, and that is the Creator's love, *Zaagi'idiwin*. For all life, in all forms scattered throughout *Gaazhige Geezhig*, the Forever Sky, is a living expression of that love.

"On *aki* (earth) the Creator took some of the earth and molded and shaped it and created life in all its diversity, from tiny, single cell organisms to dinosaurs and whales, plant and animal beings so numerous in their variety that we have yet to identify them all. And among the animal beings the Creator made the many kinds of wolves, in all sizes and colors, mannerisms and dispositions, and placed them in the great garden that is *aki* on which to run and play and hunt upon. And when all of the other things were made, the Creator made First Human, the last animal being of the creation."

—

"Were we always wolves, *Zhi-shay*?" Youngest Nephew asked. "Sometimes in my dreams I am a bear or a fish, and once I was a bird," he continued. The other young ones chimed in as well, a mouse, a mosquito, even a tree.

"I do not know if we've always been wolves. Some of the stories say our early ancestors were small creatures, rodents that ate insects and crustaceans. Over time, the stories say, some chose to remain small and became the mice, moles, voles, squirrels, and chipmunks we wolves sometimes feed upon. Others grew and became deer, moose, badgers and wolverines, woodchucks, weasels, bears, porcupine, and beaver. Somewhere along the way, the stories go on to say, our wolf ancestors developed an appetite for the flesh of other animals, and eventually divided along several paths, one becoming canines and the other felines. The felines, bobcat and lynx and panthers, are the wolves' distant cousins. Canines became fox and coyotes and dogs, and us. Dogs were wolves that moved in and among the camps of humans, eventually becoming their companions. Wolves chose to remain free, wild. And I have heard stories of other close relatives, jackals and dingoes, and wild dogs, living in distant places, in lands our ancestors may have migrated to or from long ago.

"I suppose because I have an innate curiosity to wonder of such things, one night when I was young and these stories were being told, I asked the elders what our ancestors were before they were small rodents, and thereafter each of the stories took many evenings in their telling. And if I am to accept the truth in the stories, then I would say before we were rodents we were salamanders and lizards. And before that we were fish that came out of the sea to live on land, and before that we were creatures without bones, crustaceans, jellyfish, and the like. And sometime before that, the stories say, plants became plants and animals, animals. And before that we were indistinguishable, neither plant nor animal. And before that we were tiny organisms, too small to see with the naked eye.

"I remember asking what we were before that and was told, as always was the case, to come back another evening when the stories would be continued. And so when it came time I returned and listened in wonderment of it all.

"Before there was life in all its sizes and shapes and varieties, I was told, there was *aki*, earth. And I was told the earth herself is a living being, made of water, rock, air, and fire – the original substances that make up all of earth, all planets, moons, stars, and galaxies, and that each of these four elements makes up each and every living thing. That same night, very late, when the stories had been told all throughout the evening, until it was almost first light, I asked, and what were we before we were all of that? What were we before *aki*?

"We were the matter of the very first stars, of nebula.

"And what were we before that, I asked?

"We were a burst of pure energy in the form of light, I was told.

"And before that we were nothing.

"So there I was, that night after the final story had been told, the last of the young pups that hadn't long fallen into sleep. Even then only the eldest of the wolves remained awake as well, my grandparents and an old uncle. And I, almost too tired to speak, my voice raspy, had two final questions.

"Grandfather, I asked, and what was there before there was nothing?

"The Creator, he said.

"And what is the Creator made from, I continued?

"*Zaagi'idiwin*, he said.

"Love."

—

"There are other stories, of course, of how we became wolves. Some would say we have always been. That the Creator, rather than take all the eons it would take for life to develop and evolve and become what it has become, decided to create us out of nothing to what we are today, straightaway. That story is a much shorter one to tell and goes like this:

"We were nothing.

"Then we were wolves."

Youngest Nephew had to interrupt me at that point.

"I like that second story better, we were nothing and then we were wolves," he said. "We don't look anything like frogs or fish."

I didn't know what to say in return so I just continued on with the story.

"I am not sure which of the stories to accept as truth. These are questions only the Creator can answer. I only know I was born one day, long ago, and the earth was new to me. I was just a little pup when our mother carried us, my brothers and sisters and me, one by one by the scruff of the neck, and pulled us from the deep, dark warmth of our den. And I remember when we broke through onto the damp surface of *aki* (earth),

I breathed the cold, fresh air of outside for the first time and there, all around me were all of my cousins and aunties and uncles, all licking and nudging me with their noses. And I remember I protested as best I could from all the attention I was receiving. I remember it was dark with the sliver of the moon shining through the trees and a soft wind, the kind that comes in the season of an early summer evening when the leaves are still new.

"That was all a long, long time ago."

—

Then I told them about the naming of *aki*, earth.

"So *Ma'iingan*, first wolf, didn't know why he was the one chosen. Why he was the wolf who would walk with First Human and name the new earth. He only knew he was, and for that reason he became the first teller of this story. Sometimes however, even now, given the passage of many winters, I consider how the collective story of wolves and humans would be different if the Creator had chosen some other animal being than *Ma'iingan* (wolf) to walk with First Human and give names to all that is *aki* (earth). What if the Creator had chosen deer, moose, eagle, coyote, or fox? Whole other stories would have emerged from the moment of that choice.

"This is what I know about wolves and humans. Both place high value on family. Neither is made to live their lives in solitude. Few of either ever choose to do so. For either human or wolf who is alone is really someone who is searching, for another human, another wolf. We belong to something greater, the tribe or pack. Both humans and wolves need friendship and lifelong bonds with family – parents, brothers, sisters, cousins, aunties, uncles, and grandparents. We excel only when we cooperate. And we struggle physically, emotionally, psychologically, and spiritually when we are alone. Each needs other humans, other wolves, in order to be whole and find purpose.

"Both humans and wolves care for our elders. Our young are in need of education. Our young adults learn to become their own unique beings, asserting themselves and eventually affecting the whole of our communities. And within each of our communities there are leaders – *ogema*, or alpha, of each gender. Our mothers keep the family unit cohesive. And should either of us lose our mothers an entire family may disintegrate.

"Both humans and wolves bond like few other animals. The feeding of the group and defending of territory are paramount for both. Each cares for the sick and injured. Knowledge is transmitted across generations – wolf culture, human culture. When a companion dies, each grieves. The better hunters of each share their skills and knowledge with others, especially the young. They adapt these skills to changes in geography, prey, and environmental conditions.

"And finally, in dogs, the wolves that mutually, with humans, chose each other as companions to live in and amongst each other's homes and communities, humans rely on the dog's wolf skills. Humans use the wolf's natural territorialism to train their dogs to guard their villages, and to protect their herds, they have utilized the dog's ability in maneuvering large herd animals. They have used the dog's strong sense of smell in hunting and retrieving the kill. And perhaps most importantly, dogs have focused the keen observation skills they inherited from their wolf ancestors to understand humans better than any other creature, to know their human companions even better than most humans.

"Still, when I consider the circumstances upon which *Ma'iingan*, First Wolf, was chosen to walk with First Human and name the earth, and wonder of all the possibilities, in the end there is this, the story:

———

"In that time soon after the Beginning, *ni-mama aki* (Mother earth) was new and without names, so the Creator called First Human to council and asked him to walk upon *aki* and name all things.

"First Human was humbled and honored to be the 'way-ay (namer) of all the things of the new earth. So it began its long journey. And he was in wonder at all he saw, heard, smelled, tasted, and touched.

"And as he traveled *aki,* First Human noticed that other creatures had someone in which to share their life journey. Some traveled in large groups and pods, flocks, and others as mating pairs. Still others traveled as families – fathers, mothers, and children, and others with their extended family – grandfathers, grandmothers, aunties, uncles, and cousins.

"So First Human prayed, asking the Creator for someone to share in all the wonder. And Creator took pity on First Human and sent *Ma'iingan* (Wolf) to walk with, as a friend and companion, and to share in the naming of all of creation. And I have imagined when the Creator's voice called *Ma'iingan,* he stood before the Creator for the first time and was trembling in fear and whimpering, tail between its legs.

"There he stood, eyes cast down. And in my imagining only once and for a brief moment did he have enough courage to look up, and all he saw was a bright light of pure energy, of love.

"Then the Creator called *Ma'iingan* and when he tried to respond not even a whimper escaped its mouth. And when the Creator told him of his task he did not wonder or question, for he, like First Human, was honored and humbled to be the '*way'ay,* namer, of things.

"So he joined First Human then. They were not friends at first. When he first encountered the human he must have felt a great sense of fear toward him. Here, he thought, is a predator unrivaled by any other creature, an animal it sensed had the potential, even sometimes a predilection to kill others simply for the thrill of it. So you can understand that his first instinct was to run. In turn, First Human must have acknowledged *Ma'iingan* as a predator as well, a worthy companion.

"One of the natural differences to overcome in order to get to know the other right from the start was their inability to communicate with one another. Human's verbal language is complex, a spoken language of words and sentences with which the wolf was completely unfamiliar. Wolves communicate best by howling, visual posing, and body language. They must have spent many days just getting to know each other's ways. Initially, I imagine, the wolf began to respond to human's body language. Then it learned to recognize individual words, and eventually linked the words together to understand basic sentences. The human learned to recognize the wolf's keenest sense, and the way we communicate the best, our sense of smell. For we wolves smell things long before we see them. We identify the kind, numbers, and variety of things using our sense of smell. We mark our territories with urine, and identify it by scent. We recognize each other through our scent. So maybe you can also understand how difficult it was for the wolf, given its sense of smell, to be even near Human, whose strong body odor it must have found revolting.

"With time, however, they learned the other's language. And as they traveled and began undertaking the task for which they had been honored, they became friends, and eventually, brothers.

"To become brothers they had to overcome a natural reticence to be with each other. They both acknowledged right from the beginning that First Human was the alpha, the dominant male, and the wolf the beta, submissive only to an alpha. *Ma'iingan* would never challenge First Human's right to dominance, and human never willfully exerted its dominance over *Ma'iingan*. That was the unspoken understanding they both acknowledged at the time they first met.

"Along the journey, they faced challenges that strengthened the bonds with each other. On bitter evenings they huddled together for warmth. *Ma'iingan* shared the warmth of his fur with Human. Human built a fire and taught *Ma'iingan* to respect its power. And there was a time when Human cut himself on a sharp rock, and *Ma'iingan* showed him a plant it could chew and put on the wound to stop the bleeding and aid in healing. And *Ma'iingan* used its strong sense of smell to locate other animals long before Human knew of their presence or whereabouts, and led it to them so they could be named. Human removed burrs from *Ma'iingan's* paws, and rubbed its legs when they grew sore from long days of traveling. And *Ma'iingan* used his ability to herd animals when they ran in fear of them, so they would come closer to them and name them. In turn, Human used its skill with words to offer up names. So through all of this they came to know and eventually, trust the other, and become friends. And maybe because the process of naming consumed so much time, and they found themselves relying on the other's knowledge and skills all the time, they moved beyond friendship to considering each other as brothers.

"And as they walked and grew in their friendship and respect for the other, they saw how all of the things of *aki* were beautiful, how everything was connected and related to the other, and that each had a purpose and reason for being a part of the creation. Everything is sacred. For all things come from Creator's dream. And to honor the Creator and all of creation, they gave everything the most beautiful of names.

"They named all of the many kinds of wind, sky and clouds, and stars, moon and sun, daylight and darkness in all the languages of *aki*. And in the same way they named each of the oceans, and all of the rivers and lakes. They named the many different types of mountains, plains, deserts, and forests. They named all the different grasses, flowers, and trees. And then they named each of the many kinds of animals – insects, fishes, birds, reptiles, amphibians, and mammals. They named all of the sounds – thunder, waves, wind, even the creaking of trees, and all the voices and singing of the animal beings, for their voices are the music of *aki*. Then they named the emotions as well – joy, laughter, anger, and sadness.

"And their journey of naming went on for a long, long time.

"Then when they were done they returned to where their journey had begun and stood before the Creator, who spoke to them, saying: 'Now each of you will go your separate ways. *Ma'iingan*, you will partner and multiply. Your packs will run forever through the beautiful fields and forests. Your songs will honor the whole of the earth and sky. To honor your work, and to remember your kinship with humans, the face of *Gitchi Gumee* (Lake Superior) will bear your likeness.'

"'And you, First Human, will also partner and multiply. Your tribes will forever walk this land. You will be responsible for caring for this beautiful garden that is *ni-mama aki* (mother earth). For the whole of *aki,* all living and non-living things, all plant and animal beings, are your elder sisters and brothers, all of the things that grow, fly and crawl, run and swim. All the rocks, water, air, and fire are in your care. This includes the smallest to the largest of things.'

"Then Creator said that to forever remember the close kinship of wolf and human, whatever happened to one would befall the other; for both there would be times of great happiness and great sadness, of hope and despair. For that is the way of things. And the Creator said these things that would one day become true: 'One day,' the Creator said, 'each of you will be hunted to near extinction. Each will be hunted for your hair. Each of you will lose your lands. But those difficult times will not go on forever,' the Creator said.

"'Someday you will live out my beautiful dream for you.'

"Both human and wolf stood before Creator and gave thanks, and offered sacred *asemaa*, tobacco.

"Before they left, First Human and the wolf stood facing each other. The human scratched the wolf's ears and rubbed the top of its head with his hands, its fingers going through the soft fur. *Ma'iingan* rolled over onto his back in submission and Human rubbed its belly. It licked First Human's hand and whimpered.

"'I will miss you.'

"They both said it at the same time.

"And then First Human went one way,

"and *Ma'iingan* the other.

"*Mi-iw.* That is all."

Ojibwe tradition tells us that there were Seven Grandfathers who were given the responsibility by the Creator to watch over the Earth's people. They were powerful spirits. The Seven Grandfathers recognized that life was not good for the people. They sent their *Osh-ka-bay-wis* (helper) to the Earth to walk among the people and bring back to them a person who would be taught how to live in harmony with the creation.

—Benton-Banai, E. (1988). *The Mishomis book.*
Hayward, WI: Indian Country Communications, p. 60.

CHAPTER TWO

Zaagi'idiwin

(Love)

"U NCLE?" THE QUESTION CAME STRAIGHTAWAY from Youngest Nephew the evening after I had told the pups the story of the Beginning, of the creation and when *Ma'iingan* and First Human had named *aki*.

"Uncle?" he asked again. I was distracted, busily scratching myself from some itch.

"So last night you said the Creator was made out of love?

"What is love? And what is *it* made of?"

I was still scratching myself with a hind leg, and when that didn't satisfy what was itching I went to chewing deep into my fur.

"Uncle?"

"Ummmh...." I replied, still chewing away, mumbling to myself and wondering what a two-month-old pup was doing asking about love.

"Uncle?" I didn't look up until my itch was satisfied, and then I saw my nephew and other nephews and nieces, all a huddle of fur, ears, and tails, their dark, wondering eyes looking up at me, and at once I was overcome.

Zaagi'idiwin. Love.

—

When we began talking story I started by asking them what they thought about love and what it was, and those who had listened to my story the evening before, or who had thought about the meaning of love, spoke what I had told them back to me.

"I think it's a really, really bright light," said one.

"I think it's a burst of pure energy," said another.

"What's energy, Uncle?" said yet another voice of wondering and distraction somewhere in the huddle.

"I don't think I can tell you in a word or even a sentence, or even a few sentences. I think the only way you might even begin to understand it is by me talking story. Just maybe then, maybe, you might begin to know," I replied, all the while acknowledging to myself that many adults go through the whole of their lives without truly understanding the enormity of the word, the power, of *zaagi'idiwin*. And because the young ones were also in the process of knowing the humans, I began the teaching using one of their stories.

—

"So this is just a part of a much larger story involving the humans. Maybe someday when you are older I will tell you the whole of it if you are interested, but for now this part is what you will hear from me because it is about the humans and a bit about love.

"A long time ago the Creator saw the humans were having a difficult time living on *aki*. There were a lot of diseases and accidents, and they were suffering spiritually. They didn't know then that living in harmony, attending to their spiritual, physical, and psychological needs, was required to live in a good way. So anyway, the Creator saw this and it sent a spirit, an *osh'ka bay'wis*, helper, to come down from the sky and find someone who could be taught how to live in harmony, and then bring the teachings back to the humans.

"Now like I said, the story is much more complicated than this, but the helper found a young boy who was just born and brought him back into the sky. He brought the baby around the star world until he was old enough to learn the teachings. Then when the boy was seven years old he brought him to seven grandfathers, who are in charge of watching over the humans. Each gave him gifts in the form of different teachings. Then the seven grandfathers instructed the helper to find someone to travel with the boy back to *aki*, and the helper eventually found *Nigig'*, otter. So the otter and the little boy went to the grandfathers again and were given a large bundle filled with seven teachings to help the humans live in harmony on *aki*."

"What was in the bundle, *Zhi-shay*?" a voice said somewhere in the middle of the huddle.

"*Bizaan.*" Listen.

"So the boy and the otter took the bundle and they started walking back to *aki* and they stopped seven times and at each stop a spirit came and told them what each of the seven teachings means."

"How did you learn this story, *Zhi-shay*?"

A young voice of distraction spoke somewhere deep in the huddle. I think sometimes being an uncle requires a lot of patience. I continued.

"The first teaching is wisdom. Wisdom comes from life experience, from knowing enough and experiencing enough to have good judgment. Sometimes you share it with others."

"Like you *Zhi-shay*?" a voice somewhere among the pups.

I ignored the voice as best I could. Many times in working with young ones that is the best thing to do.

"The second teaching is respect. To be thoughtful, considerate to others, is to be respectful. That's hard to do all the time because sometimes others do not show the same back at us."

"My brothers are like that," one of the young females said. "They don't show me bespect."

"The next teaching in the bundle was honesty. What does it mean to be honest?"

"I think that's when you have honesty," a young voice.

"I suppose that one way to describe honesty is when you live your values. That's hard to do, isn't it?" I replied.

"Like when my brothers aren't being bespectful," my niece said.

"The next teaching was humility. What do you think of that?"

"Is that when you are really funny? You have that gift *Zhi-shay'*," said another small voice. "Sometimes you can be really funny."

"I wish that was always true. I think to have humility is to not think too much of yourself, to not always feel we are right, or to not always think we are the best at things."

"The next teaching taken from the bundle was truth. Sometimes to know truth is to be able to see what is right and wrong."

"And sometimes when someone is always making up stuff they aren't being truthful," said another young voice.

"Then there is bravery. Courage requires bravery. Sometimes we do something even when we are frightened. That is bravery."

"Like one night I had to pee really bad and I went off to my pee place and I was so scared," said a young voice.

"I suppose you could call that bravery," I replied.

Then I heard the voice of Youngest Nephew.

"Sometimes it takes bravery to respect, to be honest, to have humility, to be truthful. I think sometimes it even takes bravery to love."

Every once in a while the young ones say something wise that defies explanation, stops me right in my tracks. This was one of those times.

My nephew. Sometimes it takes love to not tell a young, wise-before-his-time nephew that what he just said was profoundly wise. We wouldn't want it to go to his head, now would we?

"The last teaching was love. And what is love?" I asked them again, just like earlier when we began the story.

"That's like when you are in *love*," said another voice.

"That's stupid. You can't say that love is *love*." A different young voice.

"Let me tell you what I think," I said, and I told them.

—

"I remember when I was a young pup sometimes I could almost be over-come by the beauty all around me, smells, sounds, what I saw. I loved the smell of the damp earth in the den my brothers, sisters, and I were born in. And when we would come out of the darkness of the den into open light it was often so bright I could barely see. There were new smells all around – grass, spring flowers, trees, and far off scents I couldn't identify but were rich and pungent and sweet. At the same time I saw the things of the earth all around me and, although we did not wander far from the den at first, I wondered at it all. I saw crawling bugs and flying insects. *Aki* was in greens, browns, blues, reds, and yellows. The sky above was pale blue with beautiful white clouds.

"I remember asking my mother about it all and she told me that all around me were the things of the earth, of *aki*, that everything I saw and smelled and heard was born of *ni mama aki*, our mother earth.

"'Look around at all of this,' she said. 'All of life on *aki* is her children: you, me, your brothers and sisters, cousins, aunties and uncles, plants, other animals.'

"And I felt it then for our earth mother, love, warm, intense.

"'Mother,' I remember saying, '*aki* is all so beautiful.'"

"Even now as an old wolf I still feel the same way. When we go on hunts, hunts I once led, a pack I once led but no longer do, when we come across a herd of deer or moose, I am still sometimes nearly overcome by all the beauty of life around me. Even in the animals we harvest. Even in them I see the same beauty.

"That is an example of love, nephews and nieces.

"That love I describe extends out to our closest relatives, to our mother and father, uncles and aunties, cousins, brothers and sisters. Even to those who would be our rivals, our enemies.

"When I was younger and vying to be the alpha there was another young wolf that also wanted to be leader, and we fought, of course, several times, and each time I humbled him. Each time he went away from the fight wounded, bleeding from the fierce struggle in which we engaged.

"And it seemed even after I demonstrated my superiority in battle he seemed to resent my leadership. I could tell it in the manner in which he communicated with me, in his body language, the tone of his voice. So I was left with an underlying feeling I could never trust him, that if I showed the slightest weakness he would take advantage. That if I made errors in judgment in my leadership position, he would be the first to criticize a decision, the first to point it out.

"Even when we both aged he seemed to continue his resentment of me. When the time came I knew I no longer had the speed, or superiority in vision, or sense of smell to lead the hunt, I moved back into the middle of the pack and watched as a younger, stronger one took leadership of hunts. When I became ill from eating something that had sat too long in the heat and sun, I was no longer able to be alpha because I never fully recovered. Each of those times I would still feel a lingering resentment from him.

"And it wasn't until he too was humbled by age and injury that I no longer felt he was my rival. When we both ran in the back of the pack during the hunt. When a younger, stronger hunter would command both of us to go this way or that way. When we would both show submission to our alpha.

"It wasn't until he was stricken with a grave illness, and one day removed himself from the pack to go deep into the woods by himself to die. I saw him leaving that day when others barely noticed.

"I remember our eyes met.

"And I felt only love for my former rival.

"'Uncle,' I asked of him. I had never called him uncle until that day. 'When you get to that place across the river and meet all of our relatives, tell them I love and miss them, will you? Will you do that for me?'

"He nodded then, turned and disappeared into the bush."

Then I told them that there is a romantic love that can blossom once they become adults.

"You're too young right now to know that kind of love," I said.

"I'll tell you when you are older," I continued.

"I can't wait," a voice somewhere far back in the huddle.

Then I told the pups that love extends out to our Creator.

"The Creator is love, *Zhi-shay*," a young voice from somewhere in the huddle.

"That's right," I said. "That is one thing you need to always remember.

"You know," I said, "There are many tribes of humans that do not believe that wolves, or any of the other creatures of *aki* except the humans, acknowledge the presence of a Creator."

"That's crazy," another voice from the huddle.

"Yeah, that's stupid." The young one that likes saying the word 'stupid.'

"These same humans, and remember this, not all of them, think the Creator has reserved the spirit world, the land of souls, just for the humans," I told them.

"When they scratch an image of the Creator," I continued, "they draw a human."

"That's stupid," said the young one who likes saying the word 'stupid.'

"I wish I could be there when they cross the river to the land of souls," said Youngest Nephew.

"And walk toward the light and feel its love."

"And find out the Creator is a wolf."

—

We can never be sure when the young are old enough to hear certain things, but that evening, I suppose, since we were talking about love, I felt that maybe it was good time.

"Sometimes love hurts," I began.

"What do you mean?" A small voice somewhere in the huddle.

"There were pups before you," I began again. "My sister was alpha female, several winters past, she had pups, four of them, two girls, two boys."

"They must be our cousins then, *Zhi-shay*," said Youngest Nephew.

"Yes, they would be your cousins," I replied.

"They were born when the snow was still deep on the ground, just as the warming began, just as the big melt began," I continued.

"They are the young hunters now, our cousins, right?" Youngest Nephew asked.

And when he said that, I wasn't sure if I should continue to tell them the story or not, that maybe they were too young to hear it, that maybe the story may be too much for their young minds, that it may trouble them.

"We had gone hunting, all of us except my sister. She stayed with the pups in the den as a mother would often do, to feed them, keep them warm. I remember that day the rest of us left. The days had been cloudy. The spirits of winter and spring were battling, one day cold, one day warm, back and forth.

"We knew vaguely where there was a herd of deer. Two days travel there, we were away from the den, from my sister and the pups. Four days gone.

"The hunt was, of course, a success. I was sent back first with some of our bounty to feed the hungry mother so she, in turn, could feed her awaiting pups.

"I remember the day always. I rounded the corner and saw my sister where she lay in death. Another group of wolves had happened upon the den, my sister. She defended her pups as best she could, but the young females of the other pack did what they sometimes do when they come upon the mother of an opposing pack.

"I went to her, I remember, whimpering. My sister.

"The pups.

"I went down into the den.

"They too lay in death. We had been gone too long, too many days. Without food, warmth, their mother.

"I will never let what happened to them happen to you. Know that."

The pups were quiet. I could only hear their breathing for what seemed the longest time.

"*Zhi-shay*." It was Youngest Nephew.

"Yes."

"Thank you for the story," he said. "And for your promise to us."

"Thank you Uncle," I heard the other pups, repeating it over and over again.

The *Anishinaabeg* Ojibwe called the ecliptic *Ma'iingan Mikan*, the wolf's trail. *Ma'iingan Mikan* is the path the earth and moon travel around the sun, and the sun travels throughout the galaxy during the seasons through the universe, in a great circle from beginning to beginning. The wolf's trail explains the seasons, the phases of the moon, and eclipses of the sun and moon. On our journey through the universe during each season – spring, summer, fall, and winter – we see the different spirits that live in the sky during the different seasons.

CHAPTER THREE

The Wolf's Trail

(Love, Bravery, Humility)

THE STORY ABOUT LOVE HAD taken hours. And I suppose I was emotionally exhausted from telling them about my sister and the pups before them, the ones who had died.

I nudged my way among the pups, joined the huddle and shared our warmth.

Just as I was drifting off to sleep, Youngest Nephew spoke.

"Uncle?"

"Yes nephew," I replied.

"Could you turn your head just a bit the other way? Your breath, um, sometimes…"

—

The next night, of course, they all returned to hear more story, the young nephew and niece, the one who always said the word "stupid," two others who always managed to fall asleep before the story ended, a mischievous one who wasn't into listening, another who rarely spoke, and one who never asked any questions, who made me wonder if he even knew what was going on.

I started by telling them about how things change as we walk through life.

"When I was a younger wolf, before I was your uncle, I was a beta male. And eventually I became the alpha male. Now I am a mid-level wolf, and an uncle."

"You were a beta and an alpha?" It was Youngest Nephew, of course, surprised I suppose. He continued. "What happened to you, Uncle?"

"I got old, I guess."

"I'm never getting old," he replied. "Uncle, you are *really* old. That must have been a long time ago."

"One of the wonderful things about getting *really* old," I replied, " is that I have lots of stories."

Whenever I tell stories nowadays, it seems, memory brings me back to the times when I was young. I get to revisit those times again. In my imagining I get to daydream all of my relatives who have passed on – my mother, father, uncles, cousins. My brother.

"How come you remember all of the stories?" One of the young ones asked.

"Because I listened when they were told to me," I said, especially to the several I knew weren't, or were incapable of, listening.

—

"Tonight, I want to tell you," I said, "about when I was a younger wolf, and about my brother. I had a brother," I said, "and he too heard the stories.

"So during the telling of the stories when I was young, always in the background, away from the rest of us but just within listening distance, was my brother, *Zhigaag* (Skunk), the omega. The omega, the one always just outside the circle from the rest, the one at the very bottom of the hierarchy, the one who often went hungry, the one who ate last, docile, playful, always wanting to be accepted but never so, the submissive one. The one targeted for a mocking kind of teasing, even by the pups, when one asked the storyteller during the storytelling, so, does Human smell as bad as *Zhigaag*, and everyone looked off in the distance toward my brother and laughed. My brother, who was actually bigger than me, than most, who should have been a mid-level wolf, but was always aggressively targeted by one or more wolves and invariably ended up on his back, whimpering, submissive. *Zhigaag* alone held the position of omega male.

"*Zhigaag*, always uncertain, tail firmly tucked between his legs, shoulders hunched and head lowered as he moved about. I don't know why or how it was that I became what I became and he became what he was, we of the same litter, same parents, same nurturing and upbringing. The only of my brothers who would willingly approach me whenever I was near him, timidly licking my face. And during those times I was close enough to him I would see the scabs and bumps where other wolves had bitten him, the scars on his muzzle and upon him where the fur would never grow back. How many times I was witness as other males grabbed his snout the way wolf mothers disciplined one of their young ones, for no other reason other than they could. For *Zhigaag* rarely did anything to deserve it, or all the other wrongs done to him. Only during the rare times we were alone and away from the pack was he finally be able to relax, if only for a moment, and look at me with his wise eyes, knowing he could trust me, and put his face deep into my shoulder and stay there. And I would feel then the special place he held in my heart.

"My brother. Sometimes I would purposely sneak away from the rest to meet up with him, for I had to be careful so as not to show any preferential treatment in front of the other wolves. And at those times we would often simply sit together and enjoy, in silence, the company of the other.

"Maybe it was the death of the former omega at the hands of a bull moose that prompted the selection of *Zhigaag* to the role. He had once been a mid-level wolf. I only know that he remained lovable, no matter his position and treatment, always the one to instigate games of tug of war, or chase. There he would be, crouching in play stance, legs wide, butt and tail wagging madly in front of a fellow male. And the chase would begin, him zigzagging about with his mouth open as if in a smile, always nearly allowing himself to be caught, then running madly away. Finally, he would allow himself to be caught, and roll over submissively, the other wolf straddling over him in either mock or real aggression depending upon its mood or temperament. And there the game would end, my brother licking the muzzle of his victor.

"Sometimes though, when he and I would play alone, I would allow him to chase me, and in the end I would be the one who would lick his muzzle, as if to say, brother, today is your day to be victor. But the next time we played, it would be I who would be victorious, because I always had to show the rest of the pack that, even in play, I was the one who was dominant.

"There would be other occasions, however, when *Zhigaag's* playful ways would turn on him. The chase would begin, with one or more of the other wolves in full pursuit. And it was during the chase I would see what was happening was no longer play. I would see the fear grow in his eyes then, and the once playful posture change to one of fear, the ears straight back, tail firmly between his legs. Then he would be on his back in submission, and the other wolf or wolves would be on him with their fury. The next day, sometimes even sooner, he would be back for more, instigating another game of chase or tug of war, always wanting to fit in and be accepted, always hoping his lot in life would change for the better.

"The times we would gather together and howl would be especially poignant. Often it would be *Ogema*, our leader, who would begin and the rest of us would gather around him. At other times, however, someone else would begin and it would catch on until there we were, all of us with the exception of my brother, together in a group howl. At these times, there he would be alone, off in the distance where he always was. Never fully included as part of the group. And always I will remember his deep, mournful howling, as if he were expressing all of the pain and loneliness he endured in his life, my brother. Even at times such as this, one of the other wolves would somehow be offended by my brother's participation in the howling and run wildly over to him because he had the audacity to think he was somehow a fully accepted member of the pack, whereupon he would fall onto his back into submission, whimpering. Then they would leave him alone and rejoin the rest of the pack, and soon enough he would gather back his courage and throw back his head again, howling in silence.

"So *Zhigaag* remained in the distance during the nights the story of the naming of *aki* was told. Far enough away to be acceptable given his role in the pack, close enough to hear the story. Only when we were alone did he ask questions about *Ma'iingan's* journey and all that First Human and the wolf saw and did. During those times I would try to fill in all the gaps in the story for him, between what he heard and understood, and wanted to better understand. For the most part he reserved his questions to those about First Human, and of the Creator.

"'What was First Human like?' he asked. I would say the human is like us, wolves. We are alike in so many ways. 'And the Creator,' he said, 'looked like a bright light of pure energy. Is that like the sun?' he asked, and I would say,

"'Yes, like the sun and many, many of its sisters and brothers all shining as one.'

"'And what do you think *Ma'iingun* felt when he stood in front of the Creator?' he asked, and I said, 'He felt an overwhelming sense of love.'

"'My brother, that is the love I have for you,' he said.

"Another time when we were alone he told me that he had recently paid a visit to the humans. At a distance, though, he said. He lay in the trees near their village, he said. He listened to their stories. At night when there was snow on the ground and when there are only the stars, he began, they told these stories. So then, his telling of the story began:

"'The sky has different spirits during each of the seasons,' he said, 'and each of these spirits has its stories. In *ziigwan* (spring) there is Curly Tail, the Great Panther, and there is the Sweat Lodge. And he told me their stories, as well the stories of the Woman's Star, Morning Star, and Evening Star. *Niibin* (summer) is the time of Crane, Skeleton Bird, the Exhausted Bather, and *Waynabozho,* First Human.' He told me their stories then.

"First Human, *Waynabozho*, I reminded him, is the one *Ma'iingan* traveled with in naming the earth. He told me as well about the Sun, Night Sun (moon), and the Forever Sky, or universe. *Dagwaagin* (fall) there is Moose, the Hole in the Sky, and Sweating Stones. He told me their stories. And then he told me the stories of the Northern Lights, and more stories of the Forever Sky. *Biboon* (winter) there is Wintermaker. He told me its story. Then he told me the stories of the Milky Way, of Shooting Stars, and about the wisdom in the stars.

"'Finally,' he said, 'there is *Ma'iingan Mikan*, the wolf's trail. This is the path the earth and moon travel around the sun, and the sun travels throughout the galaxy during the seasons through the universe, in a great circle from beginning to beginning. The wolf's trail explains the seasons, the phases of the moon, and eclipses of the sun. On our journey through the universe during each season – spring, summer, fall and winter – we see the different spirits during the different seasons.

"'Our lives,' he said, 'also follow the wolf's trail, traveling in a great circle from beginning to beginning. Each of the seasons of our lives – baby, youth, adulthood, and elder – has its own stories.'

"I remember the story was so beautiful. Now whenever I gaze into the sky at night, I look for the spirits that live there depending on the season and remember their stories, and I think of *Zhigaag*, my brother, and of his wisdom and gentle ways.

"Even when we traveled my brother would remain behind us, away from the rest of us, the distance determined by a look, a warning, from another of the pack. Sometimes I would circle back just to see how he was. And sometimes he would sneak in close and attempt to lure one of the other wolves into play. 'Play chase with me,' he would say. 'Play tug of war with me.' Invariably during our journey one of the wolves would turn and snarl, and send him scampering back off at the required distance.

"So it was during one of our travels that we occasioned upon another pack, or rather, they occasioned upon us. Because of the wind direction when they smelled our scents they lay hidden deep in the trees and rocks just far enough away so we could not detect their scents. Then when we were at that distance where they would remain undetected they began following us. This went on for some time, I suppose. We know now that the alpha male of that group intended to challenge *Ogema*, our male leader. Maybe we had accidentally happened into their territory. Maybe the alpha of that pack was threatened by the mere presence of another alpha male. We will never know the reason.

"We got their scent eventually. And after some time, their alpha appeared, followed by the rest of his pack. *Ogema* stepped forward to meet his challenger.

"At first none of us lesser wolves from either pack stepped in to intervene in the battle, although there was much posturing on both sides. I stood at the front of my pack, ready to join in upon the command of my alpha, and I could see the beta male from the other pack do the same. The two alpha fought for what seemed like the longest time, and we all knew it would be a fight to the death.

"It was then that I saw *Zhigaag* for the first time since the confrontation had begun, behind the opposing pack. He stood there, growling and barking, posturing as we all did, seemingly unafraid that he stood alone without any support from our group. And if I could have spoken to him I would have told him to move back, go back into the deep of the woods and circle around the other pack to us, to his group. But there he was, ready for battle, proud.

"One of the members of the other pack noticed him then, alone, the beta male, and in no time he and the members of the pack were after him. 'Brother,' I called to him, 'run. Run and hide in the trees.' And at first he did, like I'd always seen him running, but this time was not play. This time would not end with him rolling on his back and licking another's snout in submission.

"I called to our wolves then to help save him, to even the battlefield, join in the fray. Then suddenly, *Zhigaag* turned and faced the beta and wolves of the opposing pack. And I saw that he was no longer acting the role of omega. He charged then, and hit the beta at full speed, knocking him over and was upon him, his teeth buried into its throat. Then I saw the other wolves engulf him, just as we arrived and joined in the battle.

"Soon enough it was over. *Ogema* was too strong for the opposing alpha male, who lay in death. His pack was quickly dispatched and left the way they came. The rest of us stood licking our wounds.

"I saw him then, my brother. He rose to his feet slowly but I could see that he was gravely injured. 'Brother,' he said. I could see him panting hard, and knew he was having difficulty breathing. 'Did you see us today, brother? We fought bravely, all of us. Did you see them run from us?' he asked.

"My brother. He sat at first, but soon he lay on his side, his chest rising and falling slowly. And then he began singing, ever so softly, the weakness in his voice barely able to form into words. And I know now it was his dream song, the one that would carry him to the spirit world.

"I went to him then, whimpering, licking his wounds, and the rest of the pack soon joined me for a while, then went off separately to their own areas to lick their wounds and mourn in their own way. For no matter the way he had been treated in the past, my brother was loved. The way all omega are loved.

"He died that day. And when he did I began mourning, howling, and was soon joined by the others. We continued to do so for what seemed like the longest time."

—

"In time, the pack left me alone with *Zhigaag*, and I lay down beside him, licking his wounds through most of the night until his body was cold and stiff. Sometimes I would rise and circle his body, then lay next to him again, as if my heat, my life, could warm his. I knew, of course, his soul spirit was no longer there, that it had left him at the moment of death and was on its journey to the land of souls. There was, however, that part of me governed by memory and love that longed for him to remain on *aki* with me, the part that had to reconcile the fact that I would never see him again in this world, never run with him again, never sit silently alone and just be with him. That he would never again, in this world, nuzzle deep into me the way he often did, to show his love. And I suppose it was selfish thinking on my part, my missing him, my grief, because I knew that his death ended all of his suffering. That his time on *aki*, the constant torment he suffered as the omega, the reality of his never being fully accepted as a member of the group, the daily humiliations, all of that ended at the moment of his death.

"And I wondered as well what might have been going through his mind when the opposing pack turned on him and their beta charged, when I saw him turn and face the attack, when he charged the opposing beta and sunk his teeth deep into its neck, when the other wolves set themselves on him. I marveled at his bravery in facing them alone, of the realization this was no longer just a chase. I wondered of his pain then as they tore at him. And I wondered when he realized his impending death, and how death approached him.

"I remember asking myself that evening of the greater purpose his life had served, of the why of his existence. Of why some of us are chosen to live to be old and why some die very young, like my brother, living out an existence that no other being would choose to live. That he was lonely and rejected. That during his life his mother and I were the only other beings that outwardly showed him love. And I had to ask myself if his life really served a greater purpose. Was his reason for being to be tormented on a daily basis? Was he put on *aki* to never be allowed to travel with the group, to feed on scraps, if there were any, after all others were fed, to sleep apart from others whether it was freezing cold or raining, to submit, to serve as a form of cruel entertainment for the others? And I guess I had to reconcile all of that and acknowledge that maybe part of his purpose and reason for being was for me to have a brother who loved me, and whom I loved in return.

"I just know in the end I saw him die that day. I saw life leave his eyes and heard his last breath.

"I left my brother sometime before the sunrise. We wolves do not mourn the way humans do. We do not, as the humans do, prepare the body for the spirit journey. We do not wash and dress it in its best clothes, laying down the utensils and weapons necessary for the spirit journey. We do not leave food to sustain it along the way. Nor do we build a mourning fire and feed it for four days, offering *asemaa (tobacco)* to the spirits. We do not bury the body in the earth in a sitting position the way the humans do, facing westward toward the land of souls.

"We have even heard that the humans' customs dictate the time their grieving carries on, of how they blacken their faces for a year to show it. That they will not dance during the year at their social gatherings. That if they lose their mate, they resume their lives after a year, and if they are of breeding age announce they are once again eligible for a mate, or mates. That there are even some, the stories say, who carry their grief with them throughout the rest of their lives, who can't move on, who get stuck somewhere in a nether land of memory, who relive their loved ones' lives and deaths over and over in their heads.

"Wolves leave the body as it rests in death, close to its mother, *aki*. A body that has served as a temporary vessel for a soul spirit, a body, like all vessels, whether they are human or wolf, or whatever kind of plant or animal being it is, made of air, wind, fire, and rock. Because we know all of that will be broken down and returned to *ni mama aki* (mother earth) and become a part of her again.

"None of this is to say that wolves do not grieve similarly to our human relatives. We do mourn for days, sometimes continuing for several weeks, our heads low and tails between our legs. And often in mourning we no longer howl as a group. During this time we sometimes stand away from one another and howl alone in our grieving. We know that humans sometimes do the same, that both their bodies and faces show the outward expressions of grief. For sometimes we hear them wailing softly alone late in the evenings.

"My brother. I just knew he no longer suffered, and I was comforted by the knowledge that when he reached the end of his spirit journey he was greeted by all of our ancestors there in the land of souls. And the Creator welcomed him. I have imagined *Zhigaag* then, in my mind, at the moment of that happening, walking toward a bright, blinding light of pure energy, and a voice, the sound of pure love.

"'*Zhigaag, umbe ingozis.*'

"'Skunk, come, my son.'"

—

"Sometimes late at night when I can't sleep I get up, alone with my thoughts. I often think of my brother then. Sometimes in my mind we are pups, playing, nipping and barking at each other. Sometimes though, we are both young adults, as we were when he died, and we are alone, with his head pressed deep into my shoulder, or maybe we are playing chase, with him chasing me, and I the one who is submissive.

"And sometimes late at night when I am alone with my thoughts, the sky will be clear and all above and around me will be the stars, the spirits of the night sky, and the Milky Way.

"I look up then. Sometimes he is there in the northern lights, dancing with all of our relatives who have traveled the Milky Way, the road of souls. And sometimes he is just there, in the stars.

"My brother.

"Walking the wolf's trail."

Do you see the path of stars across the sky? That is the Path of Souls, the Milky Way. That is the path *Nooko* followed to the spirit world.

The path leads to the Land of Souls. That is where *Nooko's* spirit is. Everyone who has passed is there.

All who are there are happy.

—Peacock, T. (2019). *The Forever Sky.*
St. Paul, MN: Minnesota Historical Society Press.

CHAPTER FOUR

The Camps

(Love, Wisdom, Humility)

THE NIGHT I TOLD THE PUPS the story of my brother, *Zhigaag*, my youngest nephew didn't ask any of his usual questions. In fact, none of the pups did. Several of them, including Youngest Nephew, came up to me just before we gathered into sleeping circle.

"*Zhi-shay'*," they said. "I'm sorry for what happened to Uncle *Zhigaag*."

And that night all the young ones pressed in close to me when we gathered to sleep, and Youngest Nephew didn't awaken me to tell me of my breath, or my snoring. I remember just as I was falling asleep I heard him say quietly to me.

"*Zhi-shay'*, Uncle, I love you."

And he nuzzled in even closer, burying his snout deep into my fur.

—

The next night, of course, the pups were back for more.

"What you going to tell us tonight, Uncle?"

"I think I'll tell you a hunting story," I said. Their eyes grew big and they sat quietly.

"And if we have time I'll also tell you the story of dogs," I continued.

"Dogs?" a chorus of voices rose among the pups. "We hate dogs, don't we?"

"Sometimes," I laughed.

The story began.

—

"I remember when I was a young wolf there were always hungry pups to be fed and their survival was dependent upon us all. And normally my Old Uncle would have been one of the leaders of the hunt, but he claimed he woke up stiff one morning and hobbled about camp.

"'What's wrong, Uncle?' we asked.

"'I must be getting old,' he said. 'There was a time I could have hunted for days, run day and night, and fought all day, two, three, or more attackers at a time.'

"The pups listened hard when he said that, believing every word. We young adults knew better. We knew he was just talking story.

"'I'll stay here today while you take up the hunt,' he said. 'I'll help watch the pups.'

"So we wondered what we should do, until he gathered us in circle and told us.

"'You know what to do,' he said to us, speaking especially to several of us younger ones. 'You know where to go to find them,' he said, speaking of a herd of deer whose scent had alerted us to their presence just the day before.

"It had been our Auntie and Old Uncle who had taught us to hunt. It was he who impressed on us the need to compensate for our relative lack of weapons, power, and size compared to bears or the panther, by depending on each other, by cooperating, by using our heads. By doing so, he had said, you will be able to harvest the elk, moose, and deer much larger than us. He had taught us to work together as a team, to look for opportunity, to spot any subtle weaknesses in our prey, to use our keen senses for any vulnerability. *Bizindun*, he impressed on us, listen. Listen with your eyes, nose and ears. Take up a good chase, he said, but also conserve your energy. Don't run too fast or too slow. When they slow down, you slow as well. When they run fast, run only so fast to keep them in sight. The herd is capable of running long distances, he said. They could easily outrun us if we give chase too soon. Remember, time is on our side. You will eventually notice who among the herd are the weak ones, the old, injured, and the young. They will tire. One of them will show it, or make an error that will prove to your advantage.

"He taught us as well about what roles we would take up in the hunt, depending on our abilities, age, social status, and gender. Who would lead the chase and who would attack the flank, as well who would go for the snout or neck.

"He also reminded us there are always mice or voles or squirrels, even rabbits to hunt. These will serve as a meal only in the short term, he said. You need to beware that pursuing a rabbit may expend a lot of energy in the process, and not provide enough sustenance for all the pups, nor even one of us. It is the herds that sustain. Save your energy for the herd, if you can.

"Old Uncle taught us to be cautious as well, to avoid being gored by an antler, kicked or stomped upon by sharp hooves. Only foolish ones will target the bigger, stronger ones of the herd. No, he said, look for the weaker one, or the one who is vulnerable, the one who makes a mistake and puts itself in a difficult position. In the end it is they who will offer themselves to you.

"So that day we left without him, the pups cared for by an auntie while their mother, the alpha female, led the hunt. Leaving Old Uncle for the first time, and as we disappeared into the bush, I saw the pups climbing all over him, attacking his tail and ears, and chewing on his neck as he lay sunning himself. He pushed them away with his paws and sent them tumbling, but they returned, straightaway, to their Uncle, their watcher.

"The alpha female and two other females led the hunt that day as they always did. Those who are better at hunts lead hunts. The females who led us were smaller, faster, better herders.

"We need to show Uncle what we have learned. We need to work together, we were thinking.

"So we went to the place where we had picked up a scent the day before and began following it. And we followed into the night, and part of the next day. Then about midday, several miles ahead, we got a strong scent. '*Bizaan*, quiet,' one of the females said.

"We circled the herd, moving backwind so they would not notice our presence too soon. We didn't want to create an early panic, to send them off in flight before we could give chase. '*Mikwendam*,' one of the females said quietly, remember. Remember what Uncle has taught us.

"We saw the herd then, off in the distance, and lay in the tall grass and bush for a long time observing while they fed. Observing to look for any weakness, any vulnerability. And after some time, several of us noticed, nearly at the same time, an older one slightly trailing the rest. That one, we said with our glances. That is the one we selected as our target that day. For sometimes in age there also lies weakness.

"The herd was grazing in an area of mixed meadow and low, swampy brush land, with only a scattering of trees. We knew that just several miles ahead of them, of us, was a riverbed, mostly dry this time of year, with plenty of rocks for them to stumble upon.

"'Follow us.' One of the females began trotting toward the herd. 'We will lead them to the river,' said the other, following. The rest of us joined in. It wasn't long before the herd noticed our presence, stopped their feeding, and began trotting in the opposite direction. We heard their leader bellow. 'Hurry,' it said. We know the language of deer well enough to know what was said. Soon the females picked up the chase toward the older doe, running harder, getting closer, with the rest of us closing in from behind.

"There was an area of dense brush and lowland on each side of the path of the chase, and the females soon moved alongside the doe, flanking it and trying to steer it off the hard ground.

"It was during this hunt that I really was reminded of how cooperation was so important. We were running as a group, just fast enough to maintain the chase for several miles, just fast enough to work the older deer, to let it tire. We had, as a group, assessed the herd and chosen the older female, one who was noticeably trailing the rest of the herd. We had, as a group, assessed the lay of the land, knowing it would be desirous to lure the animal into the lowland, where it would be forced to slow down, where it might falter in the rough terrain of the bog, the undulation of bumps and shallows, of cranberry bushes. We had agreed, as a group, to chase the herd to the riverbed, to the rocks, where the old one might eventually stumble. For we knew a wide-open meadow favored deer, even the older one, who could outrun even the fastest among us.

"Then came a mistake on the old one's part as it left the meadow in an attempt to pass and move into the middle of the herd, to be safe within the group. It floundered slightly, just enough to make our move. Almost immediately, the two females began attacking its rear legs. I joined them in attack, making an unsuccessful attempt for its neck. Several others ran to encircle it, and one of the pack members unsuccessfully tried to grasp the old one by the snout. If I could gain a firm grasp of the neck, and another on the snout, the old deer would surely falter, slowly suffocating. Without air, it would quickly cease its flight, and the fight would be over in short order when we all moved in on her.

"The females continued to lash the rear legs. The riverbed lay just ahead, all of us realizing the imperative of ending it there, before it could cross the rocks and find itself on firm ground.

"I remembered what Old Uncle had told me then, almost as if he were there that day, hunting with us as he had so many times in the past. Use the riverbed to your advantage. Sure enough, the old doe stumbled on the round stones, giving the females time to firmly grasp the hindquarters, one of the mid-level wolves the snout, me the neck. It would be over quickly. The old doe soon in its death stance, silent, its eyes bulging in terror.

"First to its knees, slowly, then to its side, I felt it gasping its final breaths. *Ogema*, the alpha male, tore into the soft underbelly and began eating. The doe was still alive.

"Standing off a short distance, the youngest of the hunters.

"Watching. Learning."

———

"After we feasted that day, *Waban Anung* (Dawn Star), the alpha female, left with two of the younger ones, back to Old Uncle and the pups. She would regurgitate her fill to the pups once she got there, ensuring their full bellies. And the younger hunters would lead Old Uncle to the kill, and to the cache we had buried for him.

"Some time later when he arrived, trotting in, we noticed he was no longer limping. Although it was probably on all of our minds, none of us said a thing. However, if we did, this is what we would have said:

"'We noticed you have lost your limp, Uncle.'

"After that day, and into the next hunt and the hunt after that we noticed that Old Uncle would always say he was too sore, or too stiff, to go on the hunt. We'd notice whenever hunt came up he would develop a slight limp. Old Uncle was a good uncle, the one who had taught us all about the hunt. He was not that good, however, at pretending to have a limp.

"I wondered for some time why he did that, because eventually, after several hunts, he returned to the group and hunted whenever we went out to the herds. I think now he was telling us, in his way, that he acknowledged our skills and that we no longer needed to rely on his skills alone. Maybe he was readying us for the time we would be the teachers, when he would be an elder who stays with the pups, when he could no longer hunt."

———

"Just like I am telling you the stories, my Old Uncle did the same with me and the other young wolves of my day. This is one I recall because it will help you understand the time when some wolves became dogs." I continued:

"This story was of a time long ago.

"Our friends, the crows, *Aandegwag*, always have accompanied wolves on the hunts. Even now we notice them flying from tree to tree as we travel, hopping from branch to branch, sometimes calling out to us noisily. Go for the fat one, some of them seemed to be saying, maybe not realizing the fat ones may be the most dangerous ones. Go this way, they're over here, go that way, they're over there, crows seem to say, always wanting to direct us to the herd.

"We know why they are such good friends. When we have had our fill of a kill, at least temporarily, it is the crows that move in to take their share. It is not unusual for us to be feasting on a kill, each of us surrounded by noisy crows, saying to us:

"'May I have some? May I? Save some for me. Let me have some.'

"So it was a long time ago that two of the young hunters observed crows near a place just outside the camp of a group of humans. They had been out exploring that day, as young hunters sometimes do, seeking to fill their stomachs on mice, squirrels, and maybe if they were lucky, a rabbit. They saw the crows, they said, so they went in closer to inspect. Because where there are crows, there may be a kill.

"They had stories to tell when they returned to the pack. 'We found some bones,' they said, 'that still had some meat on them. We found part of a deer head too. There were parts of a hide there, hooves. We think we have found the human's cache,' they said, 'maybe they were saving it for later.'

"So they asked several other wolves if they would like to go with them to the human cache and verify what they had found, to share in the spoils. And some were obliged to go with them because they were curious, or because they inherently acknowledged the close relationship of wolves and humans.

"The pair took the others perilously close to the humans' camp, to the place where they carelessly hid their cache. And several of them who were older, even though we were all young adults, became much more cautious as they made their approach. 'No,' one of them whispered as they got near the camp, 'this is dangerous. You do not know the strength and ability of these beings. They are much more dangerous than anything you could ever imagine.'

"'Come on,' the young wolves said, almost teasing the one who was cautious. 'Come on, it will be worth it,' they urged. However, several refused to get any closer. They lay in the distance, hidden in the trees, as the others approached the cache and claimed their plunder. And although the ones who watched wanted to return to the pack at once, to convince the others that as a pack they needed to tell these young ones of the danger of what they were doing, they stayed and watched as the others chewed away on old bones and bits of fur, parts of the kill most wolves would have left for the crows.

"When they left that place some time later and returned to camp they went to their *Ogema and Ogemaquay*, male and female alpha leaders, to tell them of their find.

"'We found the humans' cache,' the young ones proclaimed.

"'No,' the leaders said, 'this is dangerous. We need to stay as far away from the humans as we can.'

"'You are not to go back there,' the leaders told them.

"In the pack, the word of the alpha was final. There would be no questioning of their authority.

"And for many generations the wolves remembered and told the story and stayed away from the humans and their cache.

"But time passed and they, and generations of pups, grew into full-fledged adults, then elders, then too old for listening.

"Because we know the humans bring the discarded remains of their kill to a place in the woods, where it is left for the crows and mice, and other carrion to feast upon. No, this is not where they hide their cache. This was where they put their waste. And one day many, many generations later, another group of young wolves began feasting on the waste, and off hidden in the deep of the trees were the wolves who dared not come any closer, the ones who watched, the ones who forever remained wolves. And after some more generations came a time when the humans came to leave their waste and some of the young wolves didn't run away, or didn't run away far enough. Eventually some of the wolves rarely left the waste camp of the humans. Then, gradually over the course of several generations, the wolves of the humans' waste camp changed. They became used to feeding in the humans' waste dump. They quit hunting the herd. And because of that they became smaller in stature, their teeth getting smaller as well, docile, and more submissive. And then when the wolves who fed in the dump brought their young pups to feed with them, the humans claimed several of the pups as their own, and took them to their camps, and raised them in the ways of their camps. This went on for several generations. And when the humans were starving they ate their wolf companions, and used their hides for warmth in the cold.

"Over time these wolves changed to something no longer a wolf, but a wolf-like being. We know, of course, the evolution of a new being, a being that is a wolf but not a wolf.

"There was an uncle from this time long ago who prayed to Creator of its meaning. 'What does this all mean?' he asked. 'What is this wolf-like being?'

"For a long time there was no answer. Then one morning he awoke, and seemingly out of nowhere,

"*Animush*,' he said it, aloud, the very first time the word had ever been spoken.

Dog."

The Wallum Olum describes a journey from the west to the Atlantic Ocean, and the eventual dispersion of the people as they branched out and became their own nations, took on new names, and evolved into the tribes we know today. The journey has our ancestors as far west as California, the home of our Lenape relatives, the Yuroks and Wiyots. Amelia LeGarde, a highly respected Ojibwe storyteller, noted that at one time our people were in the west, "as far as California." The Wallum Olum tells of the encounters as they journeyed east and came upon the indigenous people of the Rockies and Great Plains, the great mound builders of the Mississippi, and eventually with our traditional enemies, the Iroquois. Other tribes with Lenape roots, including the Cheyenne, Arapaho, Cree, Blackfeet, Shawnee, and Miami, may have settled as others made their eastward journey, or like the Ojibwe moved east only to move westward in another migration. Eventually, the Lenni Lenape reached the Atlantic Ocean and settled near the Delaware River. From there, some of them branched out to the north to New England, to become our relatives, the Montauk, Wampanoag, Pequot, Narraganset, Nipmuc, Penobscot, Passamaquaddy, and others. Others, including the Ojibwe, moved north to the St. Lawrence River area in what now is Newfoundland, and then west.

—Peacock, T. and Wisuri, M. (2002). *Waasa inaabida. Ojibwe We Look in All Directions.* Afton, MN: Afton Historical Society Press, p. 24.

CHAPTER FIVE

Crossing

(Bravery)

T HE PUPS CAME TO ME the next night as they had done for many, many evenings.

"You aren't going to tell us about dogs again, are you?"

It was Youngest Nephew, of course. He continued.

"We hate dogs."

Then he barked, or tried to, and stuck out his tongue and wagged his tail so vigorously his whole body shook.

"I'm a dog," he laughed. And we all laughed with him.

Then after we had had our laugh I gathered them all in circle.

"Tonight," I said, "I'm going to tell you about a time long ago when the humans were at war, and about a long journey we, humans and wolves, went on. This is an important story so I want you to listen hard, because the humans I will be talking about are of the tribe, the *Anishinaabe* Ojibwe, that still believe as truth the collective story of the Beginning, when *Ma'iingan* and First Human named *aki*."

—

"For many generations, wolves and humans lived along the coast of a great ocean in the northwest, a place that was wet and warm. Large evergreen, mountains, mist. Life was relatively easy for the humans and wolves alike as there were many varieties of fruits and berries, abundant sea life, salmon in the rivers and streams. The woods teemed with elk, deer, and in the mountains were stone sheep. The humans sometimes warred with neighboring tribes, disputes often triggered when one infringed on the other's hunting or fishing areas. We wolves engaged in similar battles with other packs for the same reasons.

"In time, however, there was a great shaking of the earth that caused much fear among our ancestors, and the humans took that as a sign and moved from that place somewhere eastward, between the mountains to a great plateau. A pack of our wolf ancestors followed them when they dismantled their homes and packed their belongings and began their eastward journey, staying just far enough behind them so they would not see, not notice their presence. When the humans stopped, the wolves stopped. When they moved, the wolves continued on just behind them, hiding in the deep of the woods and tall grasses. When finally they stopped in the plateau, both humans and wolves lived for many generations. The land was warmer and on the open country were herd animals by the millions, deer, caribou, and buffalo. Both humans and wolves lived well from the hunts, the humans also harvesting food plants, grains, and growing *mandamin,* corn.

"Then after many generations the climate in one of its shifts caused a great drought and the land became dry and baked. Lakes and rivers shrunk, the land barren, and both wolves and humans suffered hunger and starvation. The herd animals moved as the drought continued. And some of the humans said to the others, let us return west. Life was good there at one time. But the majority chose to move east, and just a small group turned back west, where their descendants live today. Over the course of many generations, the group that returned west became their own tribes, the *Yurok* and *Wiyot* humans who live in a place the humans know as California. The main body of humans continued east, crossing the mountains onto the plains.

"Again, they lived there for many generations, thriving on deer, buffalo, and antelope. The humans engaged in war and more war, again and again. The other tribes whose lands they had infringed on were fierce and the humans were growing tired from the never-ending battles.

"Herein lies a great difference between wolves and humans, and I suppose, among all animals in the wild and humankind. Wolves kill for food, and on occasion may kill another wolf over territory or dominance. Most of the time, however, the battles are more posturing, and end in submission. Injuries happen often and death rarely, of course. We are hunters. Only the humans kill each other out of hatred, and in numbers far greater than any other creature. Sometimes even innocents suffer and become the victims of this warfare – the elderly, children, babies, and women. This trait, I have surmised, remains a great flaw in their character, and the reason most all other animals, wolves included, deem them by far the most dangerous creatures on earth.

"The plains were good, fertile land with herds as far as one could see, and because of that there was conflict over it, even though there was plenty of empty land and harvest for everyone. The wars continued. 'We need to move again, east,' said some of the human voices. Yet others said, 'We need to stand our ground, stay. We will someday be victorious.' Back and forth, the voices, and in the end, some stayed while the main body of humans continued eastward toward the dawn. Over the span of many generations, the smaller groups who stayed became their own tribes, *Blackfeet, Cheyenne, Arapaho*, their descendants still living in the area today.

"The group that continued its journey east followed a river south and east that cut across the plains. Then that river flowed into another, even larger one. The humans called the large river *meezi zibing* (brown, muddy river). And there on the other side of the river stood a great city of thousands of humans, surrounded by human-made hills, mounds built by the humans who lived there, to worship their gods, bury their dead. The humans our wolf ancestors were following called these mound people the Talega. The city was Cahokia.

"The wolves stayed back, watching and listening in the tall grasses, the marshes and lowlands, as the humans talked. 'We will send runners to the leader of the city,' the humans said, 'and get permission to cross the river.' So they selected their strongest runners, bearing gifts of hides, medallions, baskets of *mandamin*. They hastily built rafts in which they could cross the river.

"'Tell them we wish to settle in a place away from them to the east. Tell them we wish only to be their friends,' said the leaders of the humans.

"In short time the runners returned. 'The Talega leader,' one of the runners said, 'does not wish for us to settle near them, but that we could have safe passage across the river, so long as we will continue on our journey to the east.'

"The traveling humans counted in the thousands, our ancestors said. They began the crossing in makeshift rafts, the men taking turns paddling, each raft filled with women, elders, children. They almost seemed to fill the river with their presence. The Talega people were standing on the bluffs at the edge of the city, Cahokia, watching the crossing. Perhaps frightened by the vast numbers of people crossing the river, the Talega leader sent his war canoes to attack them.

"The wolves saw many humans on both sides die that day."

—

"The humans hastily retreated back to the western bluffs of the river, where they could defend themselves; still, the sounds of women screaming, children crying. The river ran red in many places. The wolves watched. Some moved closer as the battle waged, having never before witnessed a battle of such magnitude, fury. A mother ran, carrying a newborn into the reeds, the lowland, hiding from the Talega warriors. A wolf moved in even closer to watch. She could see the mother's eyes were filled with terror. The Talega now reached the western shoreline as well, spreading out in the marshland and reeds, looking for anyone no matter their innocence, no matter their ability to engage in their self-defense. Still, the wolf could see the woman, crouching, silent. The baby, wrapped tightly, awake, hungry, fussing, began to cry softly.

"The mother looked around in terror, for any noise could give away their position, resulting in almost certain death. Gently, her hand reached down, using her thumb and forefinger to pinch the baby's mouth shut, forcing it to breathe though its nose instead of crying. She then cupped her other hand softly over the baby's mouth, just enough so it could still breathe, so it couldn't be heard breathing.

"Darkness fell. Silence. She remained still that way until just before first light, then slowly, quietly, left the lowland and returned to her people up on the bluff. The wolf had watched her throughout the night, as she fed and soothed her baby, ensuring it was quiet, keeping them both alive.

"In thinking back to its childhood, the wolf witnessed something that night that had touched her memory, of when she was in the den with her mother, brother, and sisters. Her mother was going on a hunt. Stay, she said to her pups, with more of a look than anything else. The pups watched her leave. The wolf pup must have been thinking, I want to go with you. Take me. Wait. Ignoring her command, she scurried out of the den just as she began trotting away with the rest of the pack. She yelped. Her mother's ears twitched just slightly, then, turning toward her pup, she trotted back toward it, then stopped at a distance. The pup could clearly see the look from where it was. Then a quiet, barely audible high-pitched sound came from deep inside the mother.

"She knew without explanation what that meant, the look and the sound of her voice. The pup backed down into the den."

—

"The humans eventually regrouped on the bluffs and chose to move back, westward, away from the Talega territory just far enough to devise a new strategy for a future crossing. The wolves listened in on the human warriors as they talked. Maybe we will cross in darkness. Maybe we need to find an ally, increase in strength, numbers. Meantime, they built sturdy boats, stockpiled weapons.

"In time they found new allies just to the north. Along with their new friends they would travel in darkness across the river to the edge of Cahokia and make raids at first light. And on occasion large groups of warriors would cross and inflict death on the Talega. This went on for years, for the Talega were strong, resolute. Four generations of leaders came and went among the humans during this time. Four generations of raids, warfare, back and forth.

"Then finally after many years the humans wore the Talega down, and in a decisive battle they broke the city's defenses and burned their dwellings, ceremonial lodges, and government buildings. They took many prisoners, women, children, who were eventually brought in and made members of the tribe. The Talega warriors who were captured were forced to run the gauntlet, and those who survived were made members of the tribe.

"Cahokia was abandoned and all its wooden buildings burned, large fields of crops abandoned that went back to prairie grass, flowers and bush. The Talega who escaped went south and east. Descendants of the mound builders still live in the south and east today, among them the *Cherokee, Creek, Fox, Osage, and Seminole.* Once, however, they were a single, great nation.

"The humans and their new allies reaped the spoils of their victory. The allies claimed the land to the north and east, and the migrating humans claimed all the land of the great river valley and south. They lived there for several more generations, settling in peace, raising crops, and trading with their allies.

"There are always some among them, however, who have an innate need to engage in conflict, on all sides, because it seems they have a need to choose sides, to have an enemy. So when the tribe who was once an ally began making small raids on the humans, they countered in turn.

"The wolves watched and listened, the humans discussing whether they should stay and continue to war with their former allies, or continue their eastward journey. 'We should continue our journey eastward toward the dawn,' the main body of humans argued. Another, smaller group felt the humans should go south and east. Eventually, the main body of humans continued eastward across a series of river valleys on through the eastern mountains, taking one of the valleys to the dawn, the eastern sea. The smaller group chose the southern route, where their descendents still live today. In time these people became their own tribe, the *Shawnee*. Our wolf ancestors followed the main group and watched as they spread out all along the eastern sea, eventually separating to become their own tribal groups. In time their languages evolved and ways changed just enough so each tribe was unique. The migrating humans retained their name, *Lenape*. They would always be acknowledged among the humans as the ancient ones, the grandfathers of many tribes that would someday be collectively known as the Algonquin people. Those who separated and went north took names like *Wampanoag, Narragansett, Penobscot, Passamaquoddy,* and others.

"Our wolf ancestors followed a group that traveled north, the ones who remembered the story of the Beginning, of wolves and humans, and retold it around their winter fires, the story of *Ma'iingan* and First Human naming all of *aki*. These people settled near a rocky, forested shoreline along the eastern ocean.

"They called themselves the *Anishinaabeg*."

The accounts of our life that have been handed down to us by our Ojibway elders tell us that many years ago, seven major *nee-gawn-na-kayg'* (prophets) came to the *Anishinabe*. They came at a time when the people were living a full and peaceful life on the northeastern coast of North America. These prophets left the people with seven predictions of what the future would bring. Each of these prophecies was called a Fire and each Fire referred to a particular era of time that would come in the future.

—Benton-Banai, E. (1988). *The Mishomis book.* Hayward, WI: Indian Country Communications, p. 89.

CHAPTER SIX

The Prophets

(Respect, Wisdom, Truth)

I HAD TROUBLE SLEEPING THE EVENING I told the pups about the Talega, the crossing and migration of the humans who would become the *Anishinaabeg*. The story made me wonder why stories sometimes are lost or forgotten, for the *Anishinaabe* Ojibwe are the only group from that migration who remember the whole story of the naming of *aki* by *Ma'iingan* and First Human. So I lay there unable to sleep among the sprawl of pups late into the evening, wondering why the story disappeared among the other groups of humans, if the young humans who were to pass on the story forgot parts and told different versions, or interpreted the meaning of the story differently, or weren't listening, or if they had replaced the story with new or different truths.

I have heard that some tribes of humans lost their stories after the coming of the new humans, as they discarded their old ways for those of the new humans, or were forced by the new humans' rules to never again tell their own stories, and to adopt the stories of the new humans. And I also know that disease and warring with the new humans took a devastating toll, so much so that many of the tribes of humans died off completely, or lost so many of the elderly and young there were no elders left to tell the stories, nor young ones to listen. Perhaps for all of these reasons and more their stories were lost.

We wolves, we remember, even though we also were hunted near extinction by the new humans, just like many of the tribes of humans, just as the Creator told *Ma'iingan* and First Human what would happen, did happen.

I know that when I was young and first heard the stories I had many questions about their meanings, of how the teachings hidden inside the stories might be applied as lessons in daily living. I also knew the only way for me to remember them in detail was to go back, again and again, and listen each time the stories were told, even as a young adult. I remember sitting behind each new generation of pups and listening to the storytellers when they gathered to tell the stories, so I could hear them again. And even now, as an old wolf, whenever any of the adult wolves talk story I will invariably find myself there, listening.

It's important to really listen. And I think that as the Ojibwe have moved away from their old ways more and more and adopted the ways of the new humans they are forgetting to listen, that for many of them it is no longer an important part of their culture. In their new culture, it seems, everyone has an opinion, and makes it known to others.

We wolves are still listeners.

The morning after I had told the story of the humans and their crossing and the first migration, Youngest Nephew and a niece came to me soon after I had awoken. I was groggy from a fitful night of thinking hard, eyes puffy, bladder full, yawning. I needed more than anything to go to my pee spot and relieve myself, to fart.

"*Zhi-shay*," asked Youngest Nephew, "We have some questions about the stories you are telling, the ones about wolves and humans. Could we ask, sometime, to sit with you and talk about our questions?"

I was yawning and scratching myself, and I suppose a little fart must have snuck out, just loud enough for them to hear it.

"That's not the story we want to hear," my niece said, giggling.

So after that day I would find time when we were not busy with the act of hunting, feeding, or sleeping, and I would sit with them and let them fire away with their questions. And I was surprised, because occasionally another nephew or niece would join in.

"So, ask away," I'd say. Some of their questions really stumped me.

"*Zhi-shay*, you said there are the different tribes of humans, and that they have their own languages. What are the different tribes of wolves? Do all wolves speak the same language? What's the name of our tribe?"

"So why didn't the humans just stay in the Talega's dwellings after they chased them away?"

"Is the Creator ever going to get old and die?"

—

We had taken a break from storytelling for many evenings because I was away on a hunt. As the years have passed, the circle of our hunts seems to only have grown larger, the game more scarce. There was a time, I have heard, when herd animals flourished on *aki*, when it seemed we only needed to journey a while along the trail to come upon them by the millions, as far as one could see. That is no more. Now there are the farms, fields, and settlements of the new humans everywhere. Roads and fences cut this way and that, everywhere across a land that once was pure, unbroken. Now even a short journey away from our camps brings us within the signs of new humans, and the evening quiet is often broken by the sounds of the machines that carry them here or there, lights shining everywhere.

These machines are better hunters than wolves. All along the roadways are the bodies of the hunted, bloated and broken, left for the cleaners – the crows, eagles, vultures, mice. Sometimes when our hunts are fruitless we will find ourselves there as well. Food is food. And, on occasion, a wolf will become a victim of one of the machines. Where is Auntie, one will ask? Where is Uncle, the young hunter? The machines run so much faster than we do.

Now even the sky is filled with the new humans. In any given evening when we look into the heavens we will see the lights of their flying machines.

And in so many ways the Ojibwe have become like the new humans. They no longer walk here or there, nor do they travel the lakes and rivers in the vessels they once made from the outer skin of trees. They ride in the machines as well. The lights of their villages also light up the darkness, a darkness many of them now fear, and the music and voices coming from the machines they sit in front of day and night is all in the language and about the ways of the new humans.

We adults talk of the meaning of all of this sometimes. We'll send the pups away with one of the adults a ways when we need to talk things important. "Go play somewhere," we'll say.

This is especially true after one of our own has become the victim of one of the new humans' machines, or been killed by the sticks that breathe fire.

"What is to become of us?" someone will begin.

"Have our Ojibwe relatives forgotten us?" another will say. "They seem to be lulled by the voices coming from their machines. Maybe they have even forgotten themselves."

"What if they forget our shared story?"

So we will talk and talk in circles around and around, with no answers.

Just like the Ojibwe.

—

All of that was swimming through my head the evening I finally called the pups together again to talk story.

"*Zhi-shay'*," it was my little niece. "Your voice was quiet tonight when you called us to circle. And I see that your eyes are sad."

You know of course, that I have mentioned before the inherent wisdom several of the pups seem to possess, my niece being one.

"Little niece," I replied, "I have only to see all of your beautiful young faces to feel better. In your eyes I see the future."

"Now, the story." And I began.

"Tonight I'm going to tell you about the humans and some of their prophecies," I began.

"*Zhi-shay'*," it was my young niece again.

"What's an apostrophe?"

And when she said that all of the sadness I brought into circle was washed away.

"Anyway," I continued, "this was a long time ago when the *Anishinaabe* Ojibwe and their relatives were living on the eastern ocean. And the reason it is an important story is because it explains why they live here today in this area, and all along the big lake. And why, especially, they live here at the bottom of the lake near the island of spirits, and their sacred mountain.

"So while the Ojibwe were living there along the eastern ocean there were seven *praw-fets*," I spoke the word, prophets, very slowly, articulating carefully for my niece, "that came out of the water and left them with a series of prophecies about their future. Now, this is another long story, and the details aren't really that important, because, well, they're the humans and we're not, so the details are much more important to them. We wolves only need to know the parts that apply to us, okay?

"So, anyway, each prophet spoke of a period in time that would come true. The first prophet said the humans would need to move west, or they would perish. At the beginning and end of the journey would be a turtle-shaped island.

"That first turtle-shaped island is now a large city of new humans many, many days east of here." Montreal. "The last island is just east of here several days travel, the place of the Ojibwe human's beginning, what they call in the new human's language Madeline Island.

"The second prophet then spoke, and its story had something to do with the people losing their way along the journey, but that a little boy would eventually lead them and show them the way. I think that has something to do with them losing their way spiritually.

"The third prophet said that they would know the chosen land when they reached the place where food grows on water. That place, young ones, is just down the trail from here at the bottom of the big lake, in the bay around Spirit Island, in the new human's city of *Onigamising* (Duluth). The food that grows on water is the spirit, *ma-noo-min*, wild rice.

"The fourth prophecy came as two prophets, predicting the coming of the new humans. The prophets said that the Ojibwe would know the future by what face the new humans wore. If they wore the face of brotherhood, bearing no weapons, then their future would be good. If they came, however, wearing the face of death, bearing weapons, then the Ojibwe and all other tribal humans would suffer for many, many generations. And the prophets said that the Ojibwe needed to be very careful because the two faces would look alike.

"The fifth prophet told of a great spiritual struggle among the Ojibwe, that the new humans would bring their own stories of the path to salvation, and that this confusion on which spiritual path to follow would cause much internal struggle among them. We see this struggle still between the new human's churches and the Ojibwe's ceremonies.

"The sixth prophet said a time would come when the adults would turn their children away from the teachings of the elders, when the young would turn on each other, adults, and their elders. And a long period of sickness, not just physical illness, but a pervasive, lingering spiritual sickness would pervade their communities for generations."

"*Zhi-shay*," it was Youngest Nephew. "This is what we see among them now, isn't it? All of the suffering among them in so many ways, that is it, isn't it?"

"It is," I said.

Several of the pups began whimpering then. And I went to them there in the huddle and let them burrow their snouts deep into my fur.

"Uncle," they said. "We wondered why they are suffering so much."

"There are some of them that seem to think," I said, "that if they acquire more things or drown themselves in drink or drugs they will be healed.

"Then a seventh prophet appeared, and it was much younger than the others, and it had a strange light in its eyes. It said a time would come when there would come young humans who would try to retrace their way along the trail to look for what was lost. They would go to the elders, and sometimes the elders wouldn't know, or would be afraid to speak, but still they would keep searching."

"Will the humans find their way along the trail?" asked a voice from somewhere in the huddle.

"I don't think we know the answer to that question yet," I replied. "They aren't there yet. We see some of their young searching. We see some returning to the teachings of the seven grandfathers. We hear their old language being spoken more and more, and that's important because the values are inside the language. We hear their music and dance and see their art everywhere throughout their villages. We see they have scratched their values on the walls of their lodges, as if putting them there will make them live again. Real change, however, must be much deeper than that. One can speak the old language without knowing the true depth of its meaning, sing and dance to their traditional music and do the crafts. Scratching things onto walls, moreover, does nothing but to serve as a reminder of what must be changed on the inside.

"Real change will happen when they begin to live their values, when they cease trying to deaden their pain with chemicals or heal themselves by accumulating things, when they ask the Creator to help them clean out what is there in their hearts, all the emptiness, all the brokenness, the pain, all the generations upon generations of suffering they have had to endure. It is really a wonder they have survived all they have had to endure in the first place – losing their lands and ways of being and being treated as unequals for generations, watching some of them suffer from chemical use and many from poverty. So they have a lot to recover from.

"Real change requires they surrender completely to the Creator, to say, 'Creator, I can't do this myself. We can't do this ourselves. I'm tired of all of this emptiness, brokenness and pain, tired of watching generation after generation of our people suffer.'

"Only when they empty their hearts of all of that will they be able to let in…"

"The Creator's love," said my little niece.

"Yes," I said.

"*Zaaga'idiwin,*" she said.

"Yes," I said again.

"The answer is so simple," I continued.

"And so complex at the same time."

—

When the pups were a little older I gathered several of our young warriors to ensure the pups' safety and took them along the trail to a place atop the Ojibwe's sacred mountain overlooking Spirit Island, which lies in a bay leading to the big lake, the one that bears the likeness of a wolf. It was late in the evening of a full moon and down below us, spread out, were the lights from the large new humans' settlement of *Onigamising*, Duluth.

I told them that this was the place below, Spirit Island, where the Ojibwe had gathered on the sixth stop of their migration. This is where they found the food that grows on water. Here the Ojibwe had a great discussion about the turtle-shaped island at the end of their journey. And the Ojibwe who had traveled the southern shore of the big lake must have told the others who had journeyed around the northern shore that they had seen such a turtle-shaped island several days east along the lake's south shore.

"Our ancestors told a story," I told them, "how the humans camped in and near the bay where the river meets the big lake for some time before they journeyed east to their final stop, Madeline Island. They observed during that time how one of the young female humans was brought to a specially constructed lodge when she had her first menses, and a young male human to a place of solitude to receive his vision, to find his purpose and reason for being. Unlike the males, females were under no obligation to seek a vision, since in them is the ability to create life itself. This did not preclude those females who wished to seek a vision, but unlike the males, they were not obligated to partake of it. Instead, with their first menses she was brought by her mother or grandmother to a specially constructed lodge where she remained from several to many days, feeding only on water, visited only by her mother or grandmother. When the vigil was over and she returned to the village she was considered a woman.

"The young male was brought very near here by his father, to the top of the mountain and a small specially constructed lodge just for the purpose of seeking one's vision. Here he was left for four days and told to dream, to seek a vision that would give him life purpose. After four days, his father came to retrieve him."

"*Zhi-shay'*, did the boy have his vision?" It was one of the pups.

"Can you take us to *exactly* the place he was brought?" A voice of distraction.

"So, what was his vision, life purpose?"

"His purpose," I said, straight-faced, "was to have his vision quest observed by our wolf ancestors so they could tell the story of it and pass it down for generations so you could hear it."

I hoped they didn't take my version of the story, a fib of course, literally.

Several days after I took the pups to the place overlooking Spirit Island, Youngest Nephew came to visit one afternoon as I lay sunning.

"*Zhi-shay'*," he began hesitantly. "I don't know my life purpose."

"Sure you do," I replied. "Part of your purpose was determined before you were even born. It's just not clear to you yet because you are still young."

"When will I know?" he asked.

"The Creator made us, you, me, all of us here, your family. It made us for a very special reason."

"So I don't need to go seek my vision?" he asked.

"No," I said.

"Wolves do not need to seek a vision."

"Our purpose and reason for being," I said, "is to be wolves."

The Island (Madeline Island) is named after Madeleine Cadotte, daughter of Chief White Crane and wife of fur trader Michael Cadotte. The Ojibwe (Chippewa) and other native peoples made their home here for hundreds of years before European contact. Etienne Brule, a French explorer, visited Madeline Island about the same time as the Pilgrims landed at Plymouth Rock. About 1660, two explorer/fur traders, Groseilliers and Radisson, made their way to Chequamegon Bay. Five years later, Jesuit Father Claude Allouez and Father Jacques Marquette arrived. A mission was soon established at LaPointe, on Madeline Island. For the next 150 years it was an important outpost for French, British and American fur traders.

—Madeline Island Chamber of Commerce, Island History,
madelineisland.com/madeline-island/island-history

CHAPTER SEVEN

The Arrival

(Love, Bravery)

I CONTINUE TO SPEND A LOT of time wondering what the pups will remember of my storytelling when they are adults, whether they'll get the nuances, the deeper meanings of the stories, or if what I tell them will be simply stories. I think maybe I've had to rationalize my wondering in order to continue my role as storyteller. Maybe there are some who, when they are older, will revisit the stories in their imaginings, their dreams, and they will search for and find the essence of stories, the teachings. Maybe they will find the meanings when they become the storytellers. I hope that is true. I also know, however, there will be more than a few who will never find the deeper truths, who will walk through life blissfully missing the point of things, my stories included.

And that has left me wondering whether the blissful, who are incapable of knowing that there are deeper truths hidden inside the stories, are indeed missing the point, the deeper meanings? Or is the story itself, simply understood, enough for them?

Anyway, after talking story for several evenings on end, I needed a break, so I told the pups that if they really needed to hear another story right away they'd need to find another uncle.

"I need a break," I told them.

"What from?" It was Youngest Nephew, of course.

"From your questions," I replied, nudging and sending him rolling.

—

My evenings away from being storyteller allowed me to think about what other stories I might tell them, and what order, or progression. I decided that I should tell them the story of when the wolves and *Anishinaabeg* Ojibwe humans of Madeline Island were first visited by the *chimookomon*, or long knives, the large numbers of new humans who had come across the eastern ocean and settled here.

"You know there are many different kinds of humans," I began, "just as there are many different kinds of wolves. We come in all sizes and colors and dispositions and..."

"What's a diposition?" The question came from somewhere in the huddle of fur and pointy ears.

"DISposition," I said, slowly emphasizing and enunciating the beginning of the word. "That's how individuals see things. Each of us has our own ways. Some of us are always happy. Some of us aren't. Some of us say DISposition. Some of us don't. Not yet, anyway."

"Is that why we sometimes stand, or sometimes sit, or sometimes lie down? Disposition? Sometimes we're in disposition, sometimes we're in that position?"

Sometimes they drive me all *geewanadizi*, crazy, with their questions.

"Sure, I replied, "I guess it means that too."

After that, I made a mental note to myself to try to avoid using the word ever again.

"Ask one of your other uncles what it means," I said, and ended it at that.

The story.

—

"There were a group of wolves that had lived the entirety of their lives on a sacred island, a place known to them as Turtle Island, the island of islands, on *Gitchi Gumee,* Lake Superior, the lake that bears our likeness. The alpha, *Ma'iingan,* along with *Waubun Anung* (Dawn Star), his mate, and all of their relatives – parents, brothers and sisters, cousins, aunties and uncles, nephews and nieces – made their home there. There were scarcely fifteen of them and they were all family with one beginning, one grandmother, all of them together.

"It was late in the season of falling leaves and they had been tracking a deer and her two young ones near the western shore when they saw the new humans, pale ones, coming across the water from the mainland in vessels made from the meat and outer skin of trees, toward them, toward their island. And although he rarely knew fear there was something about the sight of them that raised the hairs on the back of *Ma'iingan's* neck, but he tried not to show it because he would never let the others know that he possessed fear. The wolves had discerned their scent long before they were sighted, and it contained smells they didn't recognize and found confusing. For sure, theirs were familiar smells of fire and ashes, sweat, piss and bear grease, but there were other things they did not recognize that were new to them and not of the islands, nor to Turtle Island, the island of islands. Even their muffled voices in the distance sounded strange and new and made them wonder. And once they were close enough for the wolves to discern their language, they were certain right away these were a whole new kind of humans because it took them some time before they were able to translate their new tongue to their thoughts. As they came near shore the wolves crouched hidden behind great white pines and saw they were very pale in complexion, almost like the clouds on cold, fall days, and there were several among them who seemed to have no color whatsoever in their eyes, that most had fur grown all on their faces, and the hair on their heads was many shades of light and dark. Nor did they recognize the animal skins they wore to cover their nakedness, and maybe it was their garments weren't from animals at all, for it was new to the wolves. But mostly it was their scent, overwhelming, and the wolves sensed these were creatures whose bodies never knew the sweat lodge, or the cleansing waters of the lake, or fresh cedar boughs.

"They counted seven of them, all males.

"*Andig,* Crow, called to *Ma'iingan,* the alpha male. 'We should have killed them just as they were stepping ashore, as soon as the clunking of their canoes touched the first rocks of the shoreline, as soon as their moccasins touched the rich earth of our homeland.'

"Maybe *Ma'iingan* should have heeded the thoughts of *Andig,* the black one, who had once challenged him to be leader, who still hated him deep in the recesses of his heart, who had once felt *Ma'iingan's* fury, who may have smelled the scent of *Ma'iingan's* fear at their coming, who had early on sent the thought out to all of them: Kill them. Kill them now before it is too late. Instead the wolves lay hidden and watching until the sun moved late across the sky as the newcomers set up camp, built fire, cooked and ate a meal.

"They lay there watching them for a long time, in perfect silence, practiced since they were pups, learned well. Later, as they finally left the watching place and returned to the north end of the island, *Ma'iingan* asked one of his nephews to stay and to report back to them of their doings. And when the wolves returned to their home they gathered in circle and talked about the new humans, of their coming and strong scent and unfamiliar tongue and of the fur on their faces, the strange skins covering their nakedness, and skin the color of death, and eyes and hair of many shades of light and dark.

"'We should kill them,' *Andig* repeated. 'You are showing weakness not to do this,' he said to *Ma'iingan.* 'To hesitate is to foreshadow our demise. You have always been weak that way. There is no good in these new humans.

"'These are not our brothers.'

"But *Ma'iingan* reminded him and the others that they are intimately connected to all humans. That even these strange new ones were their brothers as well, just as the humans with whom they shared the island are their relatives, that all wolves and humans share a common story. And *Ma'iingan* tried to assure them, convince them, especially the older warriors among them, and *Waubun Anung* pulled the female wolves aside, her sister and cousins and aunties, and did the same. We all share a common story, they repeated. These are our relatives.

"And later in the evening when the nephew returned he told the wolves that he had learned some of their ways, and of why they had come, and the wolves wondered more what their coming meant for them.

"And as they lay sleepless, wondering, Old Uncle, *Ma'iingan's* father's brother, gathered them all together in story, the old, familiar story of the Beginning, of the creation, and when first wolf and first human named *aki*, earth.

"Then Old Uncle reminded them that the Creator gave them the land and waters where they lived in honor of the brotherhood of wolf and human, that *Gitche Gummi* (Lake Superior) bears the likeness of a wolf's head as a reminder of their place and purpose there.

"'This is the teaching,' he said, 'and it is so.'

"So in the early morning stillness when they finally gathered to sleep in close circle around Old Uncle to keep his tired bones warm, they dreamed of the story and of their place here on the earth, and their relationship to first human, and to his descendants.

"Those we call the humans."

—

"Wolves are an ancient tribe. Our ancestors have been a part of the land nearly since the creation of the four-leggeds, and have lived in the great forests along the shores of the lake for over too many winters to count, following the great herd animals there with the retreat of the last glacier, and all the ones before that. In that early time, we seldom hungered for food, because the land provided a garden of elk and caribou and buffalo, and deer upon which to feast. And closely following our ancestors to the area had been different waves of humans, also in pursuit of the herds – humans whose names have long been forgotten, who migrated on to other places, or disappeared, or blended with other tribes. Each of the various waves of humans would, on occasion, steal one of the wolf pups and raise it to pull their belongings, or use it to befriend their children and elders, or keep it to curl next to them in the deep of winter for warmth. As well, some of the young wolves began living around the waste dumps of the humans and eventually moved into their camps. They gave these wolves a new name, *animushag* (dogs). Often the dogs would be trained to hunt or protect their villages because of their vastly superior sense of smell and sight, because what remains wolf in them is the ability to be keen listeners, watchers. These dogs, of course, would eventually become more like humans themselves, and forget many of the wolf ways which wolves had perfected to ensure our survival all of these eons. Now, most dogs seem nearly useless to wolves, only useful to the humans.

"There were the more recent humans that called themselves *Dakotah* and *Meshkwahkihaki* (Fox). Then about one hundred fifty winters ago came the *Anishinaabeg* Ojibwe, settling in great numbers along the shores of the lake and these sacred islands. They established their first village on the wolves' island home, and called it *Moningwanakuning* (Madeline Island), the place of the yellow-breasted woodpecker, the place the wolves know as Turtle Island. The place the *Anishinaabeg* also referred to as the turtle-shaped island of their prophecies.

"When the *Anishinaabeg* Ojibwe first arrived there the wolves were very curious, as that is their nature, and they crept close enough to their villages to listen, in the dark, deep trees to watch, and learn their stories and ways. Wolves learn a lot in their watching and listening, in the perfect silence that is broken only by the muffled voices of the storytellers. In this way they learned many things about these new creatures. Wolves, of course, have their own stories, and have always known and passed them down, including the story of creation. So it was to the wolves' utter amazement when, early in their first winter when the Ojibwe gathered in their wigwams and told their stories, among the stories was the one of first man and *Ma'iingan*, our grandfather, the grandfather of all wolves. And the wolves realized at once, of course, that these were the people of their prophecies, that these were the descendants of First Human, and that they share a common story, that they came to the lake and to this sacred island, Turtle Island, the island of islands, to live out the story.

"And now new humans had arrived. The nephew, who *Ma'iingan* had posted to watch and listen to the newcomers, told them these were *adawe winineeg* (traders), who had come to trade their wares with the Ojibwe for the furs of the beaver, fox, ermine, otter, and other animal relatives. And he told them that they carried sticks that breathed fire, and that the fire was a killing weapon, more powerful than any club, or bow, or spear, or teeth, and that it ran faster than any creature could run. That he had seen them take down a deer with the fire, and that the animal at once fell dead. That it did not try to rise and run from death. That it did not cry out. That it did not thrash about on the ground in its final struggle. And that made the wolves wonder of the fate of all their animal relatives, and ultimately, of wolves.

"They had scarcely been on the island for more than several days when the new humans went among the Ojibwe and offered them gifts – samples of the wares the Ojibwe had never seen before or knew their purposes, wares used to take down trees, skin both animals and plants, as well vessels for cooking over the fire because their soft teeth and weak stomachs had forgotten the beauty of raw meat, beautifully woven skins made from animals or plants foreign to them which they used to cover their nakedness, and tiny stones of many colors which they used to decorate the skins, as well to wear as decoration. Late one night as they slept, *Ma'iingan* had his nephew steal into their camp and take one of the woven skins and bring it back to their village, where the wolves all wondered about its softness, took turns rolling in it to leave their scent, and when they grew bored of it left it to the pups to fight over. They eventually tore it to shreds, as pups sometimes do, and scattered it all over the ground.

"Over the cycle of a moon they watched in the distance as the new humans established themselves on the island. And they observed how the newcomers and Ojibwe so quickly became confidants, that several of the new humans even courted the Ojibwe females, taking them back to their lodges where they exchanged the common language of lovemaking. The males of the two tribes began exchanging material things and foodstuffs – the beautiful small stones for maple sugar cakes, colorful strips of the material used to cover their nakedness for some of the cache of wild rice, a cooking vessel for the hides of deer, or several pair of moccasins.

"Spokesmen for both groups of humans would sit in council with each other most every day. We are willing, the new humans said, to trade the things we possess for the furs of certain animals, and we will give you, in advance, a weapon to lure these creatures and ensnare them so they cannot run away. And at first the Ojibwe were leery of the prospects of this trade, because their teachings spoke strongly to them that all things of *aki,* earth, are related, that the animal and plant beings are their elder brothers, that to claim the meat of another creature should only be done for sustenance, to survive, and that there are certain songs and prayers that are said when this is done to ensure the spirit of the creature is respected, that all of this is done in humility. And they knew as well, because the stories were told in every winter around their lodges that their prophecies warned of a time when they would be tempted by the desire for material possessions. And their elders reminded them of these things each day after the new humans left their village.

"Wolves know, however, that humans are not perfect beings, and that they often stray from their teachings; that although in each of them are these beautiful and gentle ways, love, that the very essence of the Creator that was given to all creatures at their conception also has an opposite. That in each and every human is an inherent struggle. That influencing them in the external world dwells an Other.

"So among the Ojibwe, the debates went on for days about whether to accept the snares of the new humans. And always the Other spoke in the ears of the Ojibwe in a strong voice for its desire to possess the new wares – of vessels made of a shiny stone that were superior to the bark vessels they cooked in, of skins softer and warmer than the hides used to cover them, of cutting tools made of the shiny stone, and even the possibility of possessing the sticks that breathed fire, which they knew at once were vastly superior to the club, spear, or bow, which could be used to quickly overpower their enemies. The debate went on in the circle of the fire as well within each individual.

"And as the wolves watched and listened from the distance they were reminded of the beauty of the Ojibwe's sweat lodge, how the individual leading the sweat would always acknowledge the presence of the Other and its power, and ask it to leave the proceedings, for just a while, so the prayers and healings and discussions of the sweat could be pure.

"This time, however, the request was not made, and the Other spoke strongly, certainly more strongly than the voices of reason, and in the end the Ojibwe accepted the new humans' snares. And when their council made its decision the wolves heard the spirits of the animals cry out in the wind.

"As soon as the spirit of winter won in its struggle against the spirit of fall and snow fell over the island, the wolves began witnessing the results of the decision. And they observed how certain animals were lured into the snares and trapped, and how they suffered in their struggle to free themselves, and how they died without dignity, without the proper songs and prayers being said. Mostly, however, they saw that when their furs were gathered how their carcasses were sometimes carelessly left on the ground for the cleaners – the crows and ravens, eagles, gulls, mice, flies, worms. That the manner of these deaths disrespected everyone and everything involved, that overshadowing the grisly ritual was a kind of greed, a shadow so dark that light would not cleave.

"And then came the day when *Waubun Anung* (Dawn Star), *Ma'iingan's* mate, along with Old Uncle, took several of the younger ones to the west side of the island in hopes of gathering rabbits and several other small animals for a feast. *Ma'iingan* knew the moment of the happening because he was certain he heard the singing of spirit voices, *Waubun Anung's* grandmother, mother, and old aunties, as well the pups she bore that did not survive birth, all of them singing. And when he heard this he ran toward where they had gone, and was met by several of his nieces, running at full gate, wailing. And he cried out his mate's name, and her spirit answered him.

"*Ma'iingan* looked in vain for her, as well as Old Uncle and one of the young ones. And then after what seemed like the longest time they were joined by *Andig* (Crow), the black one, and one of the other warriors. 'We are here to help find our sister, uncle, and niece,' he said to *Ma'iingan*, who could not hide his fear and rage for what fate had become of the three missing ones. *Andig* came to him and assured him, because wolves are family and any animosities they may have had for each other are inconsequential.

"In time they found them. From what it appeared, *Waubun Anung* had been ensnared by one of the traps and Old Uncle and one of their nieces had stayed on with her to help free her, comfort her. The new humans, however, must have heard their cries of distress and found them there. They were slaughtered in that place, their hides having been removed, leaving only their carcasses. *Ma'iingan* was wild with grief and rage and *Andig* and the other warrior had to calm him, console him. Not now, he said to *Ma'iingan*. Now is not a good time for the humans to have atonement. Now is the time to grieve and pray and send our relatives on their westward journey to the land of souls. Now is not the time for their atonement. That will come later.

"So while the other two began the ritual of prayers and songs of grieving over Old Uncle, *Waubun Anung*, and his niece, *Ma'iingan* made his way up the length of the island to a sacred place on the northwestern shore, to an outcropping overlooking the lake where through the great pines there was a clear view of many of the other islands – the island of small bears, the island of visions, the island of red berries, the island of great hills, the island of spirits, the island of eagles, and the island of caves – a place his mate and he had often come when they were young and new to love, and that they would also come as adults as a reminder of their commitment to one another.

"And he grieved there, as is our custom, repeating all the prayers and songs and singing a traveling song. Although reason told him her spirit was making its westward journey to the land of souls to be with all of their relatives who had walked on, and that she would be happy there with the Creator, where she would no longer suffer – never again feel hunger or cold or pain – the reality of her loss weighed heavily on him.

"For in his pain it seemed that all promise died with her.

"And in the evening of that day she visited him in his dreams and told him she had arrived home safely, and that her grandmother and mother and old aunties, and all the pups she bore that did not survive birth, met her on the other side of the river, and that they led her to the great village of the Creator, and that *Ma'iingan* need not grieve or wonder anymore of her suffering. And when he awoke in the darkness of early morning the sky was filled with stars and the Milky Way lay wrapped across the whole of the sky like a blanket, and the morning star of her namesake shone in all its brightness down on him."

—

"A plan of the new humans' atonement was set in motion as soon as he returned to their village. At first, Nephew was sent to watch and listen near the Ojibwe settlement and when it was time he signaled the warriors, who went into the heart of the Ojibwe settlement in the dark of night and stole away with the several dogs they kept so they would not warn their masters of their presence. And then just several nights later, *Andig* and the other warriors raided the Ojibwe's food cache of just enough of their winter reserves so they would only have enough to make it through winter. And they did this out of love for them, their brothers. Brothers who had forgotten the reasons they had come to the island, the place the wolves called Turtle Island, the island of islands. The place they knew as the turtle-shaped island of their prophecies. Brothers who had heeded to the demands of the Other, who had somehow been blinded by their desire for things, who had forgotten their relationship and responsibility to their relatives, the animal and plant beings, brothers who had forgotten the teachings of their prophets. Brothers who had forgotten the story of First Human and *Ma'iingan*, their grandfather, the grandfather of all wolves, who had forgotten that their purpose in coming to this place was to live out the story.

"The wolves waited more days and then came the heavy snows, and then more snows, and finally the deep cold of winter. And then they knew it was time and they entered the new humans' encampment under the cover of darkness and quietly stole away with their entire store of food reserves, knowing that their Ojibwe neighbors would be in no position to offer any of their own reserves to the newcomers, knowing that without food the new humans would never survive the winter.

"We wolves are a patient tribe. We have been here for too many winters to count and have observed the different waves of humans and their comings and goings.

"When the new humans died from cold and hunger, the wolves went into the silence of their encampment. And in the warmth of spring they were there again to roll in their rotting flesh.

"*Ma'iingan* was given the great honor of being the first to do so."

—

"We wolves will forever be in this land, for our spirits run heavy in this place. We are made of the very earth of this land.

"Our spirits are the moon over the lake, of the vapor of the breaths when we run hard through fields on cold fall nights with the stars all above and around us and shining off the perfect calm of the water. Our spirit is when we are tracking deer on cold winter days, of the chase and precise timing of the kill, and then sleeping curled together for warmth in deep snow, mouths covered in fresh, dried blood from our feasting. Our spirit is of the dark and wind and perfect stillness before a summer storm and the sounds of slow, rolling thunder off the lake, echoing through the trees. Our spirit is the smell of wet grass and wildflowers, and all the bright colors of the land and water and sky.

"Someday when humans are out walking in the woods, they see a wolf out of the corners of their eyes.

"And they look that way and there is nothing there."

A plot hatched by government officials was directly responsible for the deaths of four hundred Ojibwe men, women, and children, according to figures recorded by Buffalo, a leader from LaPointe. Because earlier efforts by the government to get Wisconsin and Michigan Ojibwe to move to northwestern Minnesota Territory had failed, the idea was to induce the Ojibwe of Lake Superior to come to Sandy Lake (in central Minnesota) late in fall under a guise of issuing annuity payments and rations, thereby trapping them during the winter. More than three thousand Ojibwe gathered at Sandy Lake in early October 1850. Exposure, starvation and disease led to the deaths of 170, and another 270 died on their way home.

—Peacock, T. and Wisuri, M. (2002). *Ojibwe Waasa inaabida.*
Ojibwe We Look in All Directions.
Afton, MN: Afton Historical Society Press, p. 55.

CHAPTER EIGHT

The Boy

(Love, Respect, Bravery)

"WHEN THE NEW HUMANS CAME to Turtle Island and got the Ojibwe started with trading furs for the new humans' things, that's when things started going downhill for the animals, including us," my little niece said after I had finished the story of the coming of the new humans.

I nodded my head in agreement. The story had drained me emotionally in telling the pups when the Ojibwe had heeded the influence of the Other rather than their teachings. Things haven't been the same since.

"I like how the wolves kicked butt on the new humans because of what they did to *Waubun Anung*, the uncle and pup, when they stole their food so they starved," said a voice from somewhere in the huddle. Then he continued, "And then rolled around on them come spring."

"Yeah, our ancestors were the bomb," came another voice from the huddle that made me wonder what "the bomb" meant, if the pup knew, and how he knew.

—

Youngest Nephew and the other pups sometimes mistakenly assumed that wolves and dogs were always enemies. While that was sometimes the case, it didn't always hold true. It was, however, a complicated relationship. After all, dogs were once wolves who had moved in with, or were captured by, the humans as pups, and lived in the camps of humans as their companions. While wolves sometimes attacked and killed dogs, for the most part we felt sorry for them because they had forsaken their wolf identity and its inherent freedom and allowed human masters to rule over them. Wolves chose to retain their wolf identity and be their own masters.

There have been many instances where wolf and dog got along swimmingly, and occasions where wolf and dog partnered and produced offspring.

So one night I thought I would set the record straight again and tell the pups about a wolf and its half dog, half wolf son, and how they used their wolf skills to help their human master.

—

"*Ma'iingan* was born into a litter of four: a sister and two brothers. His mother was a village dog, who wasn't really 'owned,' as the humans call it, by any one family. During his growing up, they lived with and back and forth among several families in the Ojibwe village of *Miskwabekong* (the place of the red cliffs) in what is now northwestern Wisconsin along the south shore of Lake Superior, with a set of grandparents and several of their families. When *Ma'iingan* and his brothers and sister were old enough to remember, they would be told they were born under the porch of the government agent's house, which was almost halfway between the multiple residences of their owners.

"While his brothers and sister inherited their mother's side, the dog, *Ma'iingan* entered the world with many of the physical and behavioral traits of his father, a wolf, so much so that the villagers who did not know him by name often called him 'wolf dog,' and that made perfect sense since he was, indeed, a wolf-hybrid, the product of a domestic mixed breed mother and captive wolf father. It seems, however, that he inherited just enough from each, enough dog to be beholden to his Ojibwe human alpha or master, enough wolf to retain a certain wild, quiet resistance, a yearning to be free.

"'Wolf dog,' the villagers who didn't know him by name would say to him, even when he was a young pup, and if he could have spoken aloud in their language he would have told them his wolf story, because he knew it. Dogs – few of them know their story. Their story becomes lost in the story of their human owners. I am this human's dog, one says. I am that human's dog, another says. None of that speaks to the dog's own story. Wolves know their story. Here was his:

"His *'way ay* (namer), the young Ojibwe boy who raised him, who would eventually become his alpha, named him *Ma'iingan*, without even knowing the name was part of his ancestry. Maybe he saw something in the young pup. Maybe because he was bigger and stronger than his brothers or sister, maybe because he had his way with his mother's milk before they did, maybe because he comfortably took on the look and demeanor of his father, the wolf. His father: the wolf who seemed to live fluidly between the village and surrounding forests, who was never quite comfortable being owned by anyone, who was sometimes seen in the company of his wolf relatives, who preferred to live a solitary life, who did not bark often, who did not wag his tail, who did not run happily to greet his human owners, who rarely spoke. Who was a watcher, a keen observer to all the subtleties and deeper meanings of the things around him.

"Who when he did speak told his wolf story going back over many thousands of generations: that his line was of the wolves of Turtle Island, the island of islands, the place known to the Ojibwe as *Moningwanakaning* (the place of the yellow-breasted woodpecker), Madeline Island, the sacred place, the place of secrets. 'We are descendants of the great wolf, *Ma'iingun*, your namesake,' he said, 'who led a rebellion of wolves with the arrival of the first French traders, the new humans as they called them, to the island. The traders, and soon the Ojibwe, began the wholesale slaughter of the animals for their furs until they were almost completely gone, until there was only silence, until the forest wept. You are the descendant of the she-wolf, *Waubun Anung* (Dawn Star), alpha mate of *Ma'iingan*, who was the first wolf slaughtered by the new humans. You are the descendant of a long line of wolves who have been in this place of water and islands for countless generations, who followed the great herd animals to this place with the retreat of the last glacier, and the one before that, and before that.'

"And he told *Ma'iingan* as well the story of the creation, of when First Human and wolf walked together as brothers over the face of the earth and named all of the waters and islands and hills, the plants and animal beings, and that was also *Ma'iingan*, his grandfather, the grandfather of all wolves. That through prophesy human and wolf share a common destiny. That the Creator gave us the land and waters of their dwelling in honor of the brotherhood of wolf and man, that *Gitche Gummi* (Lake Superior) bears the likeness of a wolf's head as a reminder of the wolf's place and purpose there. That there is a reason wolves live near and among the humans.

"'This is the teaching,' he said, 'and it is so. Wolves, he said, we have a story.'"

———

"So obviously, while *Ma'iingan* was half dog, he identified mostly with the wolf in him, though it's not that he denied his dog side. He deeply cared for his multiple human owners, especially the elderly grandparents and the boy, and having that faith and loyalty in one's human owners was definitely part of his dog side. That sense extended out to the greater village as well because; all of the village's 'pets,' as they were sometimes referred, whether they were dog or wolf, cared for the wellbeing of their owners. And like many 'pets,' what they sensed in their Ojibwe owners was that they were going through a difficult and troubling time, that they were experiencing a period of great uncertainty and transition in the community, and that it was not just one thing that could explain why they seemed out of balance, because the troubles the Ojibwe were having just seemed to be multiplying and feeding on one another all at the same time. Mostly what he sensed was almost a frenzy of despair, of grieving, of a village under siege with itself. And he sensed the reasons for this could all be tied to the coming of the new humans. And while it may be unfair to link all of their troubles to one thing, in this case it seemed to be true.

"While once the forests and lakes had forever provided for them, now there was not enough meat, not enough deer or rabbit, or even mice to harvest for nourishment. The circle of the hunts had grown much larger. Humans and wolves worked twice as hard for a single kill, if they were so fortunate. The animals whose furs were most prized by the French, and later the Americans, were scarce, so the balance of things had tipped. His Ojibwe relatives, who once harvested the animals prized for their furs, were suffering. And at the same time the new humans' government had confined the Ojibwe into small areas upon which they were to live and make a livelihood, on bog and wetland or clay and rock with weak soils that didn't sufficiently support their gardens. On land far removed from the wild rice lakes, which had been their primary source of food. They were quickly trading their hide and bark round lodges for the square, wooden dwellings of the new humans, their hide clothing for cloth, their moccasins for boots made from the hides of cattle. And now especially in this village, more so than others, it seems they had even traded the manner in which they worshiped the Creator, as the people had divided themselves into camps of those who worshiped the old way and those who had adopted the way of the new humans. And each said theirs was the only way and insisted the other was wrong, and this had divided families and the community in a way it had never been before, an intolerance so far removed, so opposite and contradictory from the love and grace exemplified by the same Creator in whom they both worshiped.

"And now the Ojibwe, who over the course of the fur trade had grown dependent on the wares of the new arrivals, who were lured by the desire to possess things – the vessels for cooking, blankets, clothing, mirrors, furniture, metal stoves, money, guns, and now, alcohol, were now also dependent upon the government of the new humans for food rations. For when the forest was emptied of the prize furbearing animals, they could no longer supply the traders with furs, and their access to the things the settlers possessed dried up. Now they were trading for the land, the earth itself, and it was not an equal trading relationship between the two, because the government of the new humans knew that without food rations the Ojibwe would perish from starvation. So it seemed, at least from *Ma'iingan's* perspective, that a once mighty nation had been humbled, and was crumbling before his very eyes. And the 'pets,' as they were referred to, could only watch in silence because they knew what happened to the Ojibwe would also beget them. That was the teaching.

"For several winters the Ojibwe had gathered by the thousands from all of their scattered villages on Turtle Island, the island of islands, to collect the annuities (small amounts of paper they called money, which was traded for things) and food rations from the government of the new humans that they had exchanged for the land. For land now quickly being peopled by families of new humans, the good land with rich soil for growing their crops, the good land bordering rivers and lakes upon which they could easily travel by boat and canoe. The land upon which they had brought their cattle and sheep, the land upon which they were now killing wolves because wolves saw the cattle and sheep as food to be harvested.

"Now, the government of the new humans had told the Ojibwe that the annual settling of annuities was to be moved to a place many days west, that if they were to receive the food they needed to survive the coming winter, they would have to travel there to get it. And in the village many of the adults and their children were readying for travel, and decisions were being made regarding who would go and who would stay, provisions were being gathered – dried meat, corn, wild rice, and plans made for the route of the journey, and who would travel with whom, and how long they would be gone. So, in the extended family of *Ma'iingan's* multiple owners, it was decided that the two younger families would do the westward journey, leaving the grandparents. And among those making the journey were the parents and little boy who was *Ma'iingan's* 'way ay (namer), who owned him, who was no more than ten winters in human age, who *Ma'iingan* had spent nearly every day the entirety of his three years on the earth in the company of, and whose life he had sworn to protect.

"So he watched as they readied for the journey, and he spent all of his waking time with the boy because he wanted to make the journey with him, and feared that if he left his side the boy would leave without him.

"'Take me with,' he said, speaking through his eyes to the boy. 'My keen sense of smell and hearing and sight will be useful to you and the family as you journey. My speed and endurance and teeth will protect you from any enemies. I will curl next to you in the cold evenings for warmth.' And if he could have spoken aloud in the boy's language, his pleading would have shouted it out, 'Take me with you.'"

"On the day of their leaving, however, the boy came to him as he lay in front of the family lodge.

"'You stay here,' he said to him. 'You stay right here and protect our elders. They need you here to protect them from our enemies. They need you to keep them company and offer warmth in the cold evenings.'

"And in his heart *Ma'iingan* protested because he wanted to be with the boy, to protect him, and he must have sensed it.

"'No,' he said. 'You stay here.'

"And to emphasize the certainty of his order he used his open hand to push *Ma'iingan* away, and he was left stunned and disappointed and angry.

"Then as the people gathered and the travelers began leaving in their canoes he ran to be with the boy, to be by his side, and the boy was forced to run *Ma'iingan* off many times, and finally resorted to using a stick to drive him away, even knowing in his heart it was not right.

"'Go home,' he said, I hate you, dog.'

"And he repeated it over and over again. 'I do not want you with. You stay here.'

"And finally, heartbroken, believing for just that moment what he was saying was true. *Ma'iingan* finally relented, and defeated, walked slowly back to the family lodge with his head down.

"'I hate you,' the boy had said. 'I do not want you,' was all *Ma'iingan* could think.

"From then on he spent most days laying in wait in the front of the lodge. And the grandparents, whom he was left to protect, waited with him, as he lay at their feet and they scratched and stroked his ears and neck, and face, and scratched his belly to comfort him, and he snuggled in close to them to keep them warm and let them know that he was there to be their protector.

"'*Ma'iingan*,' they said to comfort him, 'the boy meant no harm in chasing you off. You have no place in their journey. You have not traded the land for food. You have no need for the new humans' money. Your place is here with us.'

"But at night when he lay alone in front of the flap of the opening of the lodge, he dreamed of the boy and his parents, and wondered of their journey, and worried for them. And waited."

—

"They had been gone for many evenings. And one day a young runner, a stranger, came into the village, scared and tired and hungry and out of breath. And you could see even though he was strong and had a strong voice that he was deeply troubled by what he was about to tell the villagers, and his voice was breaking as he spoke.

"'I am from a village to the west,' he began, as he followed the proper protocol of telling all about his family, and clan, even though he hungered and was in need of rest, and had come to deliver somber news.

"'Your families are in danger,' he said to those who had remained there in the village. 'The rations did not come. Then came the snow and cold.

And now your people are making their journey home on foot, but there are many among them who are suffering from hunger and disease and cold. Already many have perished. They sent me here to tell you to come to them, to bring whatever food you have, to help to bury the dead.'"

"And *Ma'iingan* was with the grandfather when he first heard the news and they quickly returned to the lodge to tell the grandmother, and then they gathered as a village in its center and the people talked about what they must do. Only a few strong men and women had been left to care for those who had stayed, and there were those who were very young or elderly, or infirmed, or those who could not travel because of injury.

"'Who will go,' they all asked, and all said they would. And they argued about it for a long time, and all the while the 'pets,' as they referred to them, had already made decisions about who among them should be making the journey of rescue. Because they had that sense about who was strong enough to make such journeys, because they knew full well this was not the time to waste debating who would not go or go.

"And the boy, who *Ma'iingan* loved, who had raised him from a pup, who had named him, was all he could think about.

"The village finally decided that a few strong men and boys would go, as time was of the essence and there were not enough provisions for a larger party to make the journey.

"'Where are our people?' they asked the stranger. 'Where will we find them?'

"The reply came that, the last he was aware, many were on the western end of the big lake, Lake Superior, and they were camped out waiting for warmer weather to melt some of the snow, trying to hunt for food, and tending to the sick.

"'They will not be able to make their return without assistance,' he said. 'They will surely perish there if no help comes to them.'

"As those who were selected for the journey hastily made their preparations, *Ma'iingan* made his way to the far side of the village to where his father, the wolf, lived with the boy's father's old uncle. He found him there sunning, the old man scratching his ears.

"They walked away from the old uncle so they could speak. 'Father,' he said, 'the boy.' He was so distraught he was tripping over his words. 'The boy needs our help.'

"And then he asked his father to do the journey with him to find the boy and his family, to make the rescue, to keep them warm, to protect them from enemies, to assure their safe return.

"His father was, however, not easily swayed by *Ma'iingan's* plea for help.

"'Maybe,' he said, 'it is not our place to interfere in the course of things, in the playing out of the people's story. Maybe this is the way things should be, maybe if we alter the way of things we will only delay the people's demise, and they will only suffer more, and longer, for many more generations. Maybe it is the Creator's wish to call them to the land of souls so they will suffer no longer.'

"'Father, the boy,' *Ma'iingan* said. 'He is just a boy. He had no say in the decisions to slaughter the fur-bearing animals so the people could possess things, no say in the decisions to trade the land for food, no say in deciding whose manner of worshipping the Creator is right or wrong. He is just a boy, and I am sworn to protect him, my *'way ay*, namer. And it is not our place to wonder what will become of the people in the future. We can only live for now, for what is happening now. And what we have in front of us now is a little boy and his family, and other families, who will surely perish without our help. That is all that should concern us now. Father, please.'

"And *Ma'iingan's* father, the wolf, who seemed to live fluidly between the village and surrounding forests, who was never quite comfortable being owned by anyone, who was sometimes seen in the company of his wolf relatives, who preferred to live a solitary life, who did not bark often, who did not wag his tail, who did not run happily to greet his human owners, who rarely spoke. Who was a watcher, a keen observer to all the subtleties and deeper meanings of things, said he would help *Ma'iingan* get the boy and his family.

"And with that decision began the journey to rescue them."

—

"'Father, when will we set out?'

"'Now,' he said.

"They knew this would be a difficult journey, a journey over several days into strange territory. There would be constant danger of attack from other wolves whose territories they would infringe upon along the way, of the possibility of hunger given the scarcity of animals in which to harvest, of the snow they would encounter, of cold. And they also knew they would have to travel without the humans, the men and boys from the village who were also making the journey on foot, because they would only hold them up. For wolves are much faster. Their eyes and noses and ears are much keener.

"So they set out.

"'We will follow the hills along the lake,' said the father, 'always keeping the lake within view. And we will travel in the darkness, stopping only to rest and gather whatever food we can for energy. We will not challenge other wolves that may confront us. And if confronted, we will request permission for safe travel through their territory.'

"Then, traveling westward they went, running, running. At first light they stopped for water and were able to catch a vole and mice. Then to sleep, too tired to dream. Then awakening to wait for dusk to come, to wait more, then finally at sunset, just when they were about to lose patience, they set out again. Running, running. Then again at first light they rested again. The ground now had a dusting of snow. Again, hunting for whatever they could, this time they were rewarded with the partial remains of deer. Then to sleep, again too tired to dream.

"On the third night they heard other wolves calling in the distance.

"'Quiet,' the father said to *Ma'iingan*. They stopped for a moment, then ran a wide arc to avoid them where they could hear the voices. Running in silence, broken only by their hard breathing, the vapor from their breath trailing from their nostrils, from the hot dampness of their fur. Running, running. Then it was dawn again. Now the snow was up to their ankles.

They knew, however, that was when the mice sometimes were careless, thinking that if they could not be seen that they would somehow be safe. Wolves, however, can hear through the snow. They feasted on mice that day. They ate snow. They slept, ragged dreams. The boy. *Ma'iingan* imagined him suffering.

"On the fourth night they came upon an encampment hidden deep among a grove of cedar and hemlock. They approached cautiously, alert.

"'Quietly,' *Ma'iingan's* father warned. The camp was in darkness, without fire or any sounds of humans. His father was the first to put his head into a makeshift lodge, hastily cut from saplings and covered with cedar boughs. And then *Ma'iingan* saw them – two adults and two children, their lifeless, frozen bodies laying cuddled together, wrapped in a blanket of rabbit skins.

"He turned and motioned his father to leave this place. They did not take the time to wonder of their fate.

"Running, running. Late into the night they were running in complete darkness, the sky covered with a blanket of thick clouds, a new moon. They ran down a deep ravine and to the top of a rise. Then they could hear them. Wolves.

"'What shall we do?' *Ma'iingan* asked his father.

"'Be still,' the answer. So they lay motionless under some balsam saplings, breathing hard from running, their fur wet and steaming. And they knew now they had probably already been discovered.

"Then almost suddenly, they were there in front of them: two males, two females, and a juvenile.

"The alpha male spoke. 'What tribe are you? This is our land.'

"*Ma'iingan's* father spoke for them. 'We are the descendants of the wolves of Turtle Island, the island of islands, the sacred place, the place of secrets. We are descendants of the great wolf, *Ma'iingan*, my son's namesake,' he said, 'who led the rebellion of wolves with the arrival of the new humans. And we are the descendants of the she-wolf, *Waubun Anung* (Dawn Star), alpha mate of *Ma'iingan*, who was the first wolf slaughtered by the new humans. We are on a journey, and request safe passage through your land. We mean no harm.'

"The alpha male spoke again. 'Why should we believe your story? How do we know you have not come here to feast upon our bounty, to challenge us? You know as well the fate of wolves like you who run without the pack, daring to infringe upon other's hunting lands.'

"And all the while the other wolf was speaking, *Ma'iingan's* father was secretly sending his thoughts to his son. Prepare to run. When I motion you to do so, run like you have never run before. Run hard and do not look back, even though your lungs are burning and feel like they will burst.

"Then just as suddenly he motioned and they were off. His father's speed amazed *Ma'iingan*. And he was hard on his tail, the other wolves chasing just behind them. Running hard, harder than he had ever run. Not looking back. His lungs burning, burning, running for what seemed like an eternity. His father sending his thoughts to him, run hard. Run hard. Think of the boy. Put his face in your thoughts, only the boy. Now run toward your thoughts.

"And he did. He ran toward his thoughts, ran until the other wolves tired of the chase, until they reached the outer fringe of their territory, until the soft light of dawn began creeping over *aki*. And then they ran some more.

"Then finally, beyond exhaustion, they stopped. Too tired to find food, they both fell into a hard sleep. To sleep and dream of the chase, of running.

"They slept briefly. 'We're almost there,' his father said to *Ma'iingan*. Then they were up, sore and aching, and off again. Running, running in full daylight, they were close, running.

"Off in the distance they could see the bottom of the big lake, the great hills that mark its beginning, and the sacred mountain of their Ojibwe relatives. Running, running. They trod the thin ice across a river, past the island of spirits the Ojibwe speak of in their prophecies. To the boy whose scent *Ma'iingan* could discern, who he knew was alive, whom he had sent out his thoughts to, I am coming to you. I am almost there.

"There were several encampments along the ridge of the mountain and they silently walked along the fringes of each one looking for the boy and his family. There were fires at some of them, but others were dark and cold and spoke of death. They did this while the sun moved across the lake and warmed the land.

"The boy's scent was stronger now. Put his face in front of you, *Ma'iingan's* father reminded him. Run toward your thoughts.

"And he did.

"Again, they came to an encampment, and this time he knew they had found him. He ran at full gate toward a makeshift shelter, around a dwindling campfire.

"And there he was, the boy.

"He jumped on him and licked his face, wagging his tail so hard his whole body was shaking back and forth, back and forth, the dog in him. The boy hugged him and spoke his name.

"*Ma'iingan's* father stood back at the opening of the shelter, composed, the wolf.

"The joy in their meeting seemed to go on for the longest time and when it was over *Ma'iingan's* father sent his thoughts to him. 'The boy,' he said, 'his father is dead. And his mother, she is dying. And the boy is cold and hungry.

"He again sent his thoughts to *Ma'iingan*. I will stay here with the boy. You secure us some food. And he did as he requested, leaving, even though he did not want to put the boy out of his sight. He went in search of food.

"In his life *Ma'iingan* had become convinced there are times when the Creator walked right alongside him, and that day was certainly one of them, for *Ma'iingan's* hunt was successful and a rabbit soon offered itself to him, which he brought back and laid in front of the boy.

"They stayed in that place for days, his father and him taking turns with the hunt, for rabbits, mice hiding under the snow, carrion. Their hunger even led them to raid the waste dumps of the new humans. One time they were rewarded with small birds, a woodchuck hiding deep in some deadfall. They stayed as the boy gained strength. They stayed while he buried his father and mother in the proper way, while he kept a mourning fire, and said the songs and prayers for the dead, and mourned for them for four days, as is their custom. They stayed at a distance from the encampment during these proceedings, as is our teaching. For neither wolves nor dogs have any business with the ceremonies of humans. We wolves have our own prayers and songs, our own ways.

"And then, when all was done, they took him home.

"The boy. *Ma'iingan's 'way ay* (namer), the young Ojibwe boy who raised him, who became his alpha, who named him *Ma'iingan*, without even knowing the name was part of his ancestry. Who saw something in him as a young pup. Who saw that maybe *Ma'iingan* was bigger and stronger than his brothers or sister, that maybe because he had his way with his mother's milk before they did, maybe because he comfortably took on the look and demeanor of his father.

"The wolf."

—

"So Uncle, what happened to that wolf captive and wolf dog who saved the young human?" Several voices coming from somewhere in the huddle, ears twitching, pupils large and shining.

"The boy's grandmother gave each a large slab of meat when they returned to the village with the boy, and whenever there was any extra they didn't just get the scraps. They got the best, largest chewing bones. And whenever the grandfather returned from fishing on the lake he always gave each of them a nice fish. Neither slept outside anymore. Each was given a spot to lie upon hides just inside the entrance of the lodge, were always warmed by a fire.

"Each of them lived until they were very old and fat."

"That was a pretty good story, Uncle." Multiple voices spoke.

"You're starting to get fat as well, *Zhi shay'*, and you're already really old," said a young voice who had acquired his uncle's way of teasing.

I was pulling 'bagas (rutabagas) and carrots and beets that day, all day. I got through a little after four (four o'clock in the afternoon) somewhere. We had passed down by the church, by the Indian village, when sparks fell all around big as balls, some of them. You could see the fire flying all around us. The fire was right close to us, just about a half mile away from us…and the wind so strong that it caught up with us pretty near before we got down to the church. You could hear it crackling and sparks coming over us.

—Testimony of Joseph Petite, a resident of the Fond du Lac Reservation in Minnesota, to the United States Railway Administration in 1921 regarding the Fires of 1918, in Peacock, T. (1998).
A Forever Story: The People and Community of the Fond du Lac Reservation.
Cloquet, MN: Fond du Lac Band of Lake Superior, p. 79.

CHAPTER NINE

The Place by the River

(Respect, Bravery)

"So, HAVE YOU THOUGHT OF any lessons you may have learned from the story about the boy who was rescued by the wolf and wolf dog?" I asked when I brought them together another evening.

"I think maybe dogs ain't always bad," a voice somewhere in the huddle, who continued, "not all the time anyway."

"I think maybe what I learned is that we need to take care of each other," said another voice. "The wolves, the Ojibwe."

"How might the humans help us today?" I asked.

"Just leave us be. Wolves," replied the one who most of the time said the word 'stupid.'

"How might we help the humans?" I asked.

"Maybe by example," Youngest Nephew said. Then he continued, "Maybe just by being who we are, wolves. Maybe if we remain what we are they will remember to be Ojibwe."

—

I changed topics then to what I wanted to tell them about in the evening's story.

"I'm going to talk about fire tonight, and maybe a bit about humans and how they play. The two may seem unrelated, but in the story they tie together."

It is difficult to explain fire to those who have never seen it before, even to adults, much less to pups. I thought, however, it was important to tell them about it, because of the inherent danger it can pose to them. My understanding of fire is that it is a spirit made of air with heat so intense it burns things near it, and in its greatest fury creates its own wind, clouds. I have heard it is made of the sun and somehow has made its way down to *aki*.

Humans have captured fire. They use it to keep warm as well to soften meat and many plants because they have forgotten the beauty of eating their food raw. I don't know how they somehow overcame their fear of it, or if they ever did.

I just know that if and when the pups ever encounter it on their way along the trail, they will need to respect it, fear it.

The story.

—

"There was a group of wolf ancestors that lived near where we live today, on the side of a hill overlooking the river in *Nagachiwanong*, the bottom of the lake. The wolves lived upriver from a village of the Ojibwe, a day's journey inland from the big lake, *Gitchi Gumee*.

"The Ojibwe hadn't always lived there. There had been other humans, Dakota, who had lived there before, and before that other humans whose names are long forgotten. The Ojibwe had earlier lived on the big lake for several generations, but when the new humans arrived they were forced to move inland because the new humans' preferred to live near the lake."

"How come the new humans got to tell the Ojibwe what to do and where to live?" asked a young, slightly confused voice somewhere in the huddle.

"We've talked about it some," I reminded them. "How the Ojibwe got involved in trading furs and grew accustomed to the new humans' things, and how that grew to dependency on food once the supply of furs was diminished. Also, the new humans arrived here in overwhelming numbers, carrying the sticks that breathe fire, weapons far superior to anything possessed by the tribes here. They killed much of the food supply, and put the tribal people on marginal lands where crops couldn't grow. They brought diseases with them to which tribes had no immunity, killing them by the millions. Now today, even though there are some in government who claim the Ojibwe and other tribes make all their own decisions, in truth they are still very limited in many ways and under the close eye of the new humans' government. That's a whole other story though."

"It isn't fair, Uncle," the young voice replied.

"None of that has anything to do with being fair. *Bizaan*, quiet now," I interrupted.

The story.

———

"The wolves and humans have generally lived in peace in close proximity to each other. We know, however, that one reason for this is that wolves rarely show themselves to the humans.

"Why do you think wolves rarely show themselves to humans?" I asked.

"'Cause we're real shy and stuff and sometimes they can be really noisy," one voice in the huddle said.

"'Cause humans *are* scary," another voice said somewhere in the huddle.

"That's right, humans can be very scary," I repeated back to them. "Never forget that. Humans can be very dangerous. They are the most dangerous of all animals on *aki*.

"And why is that?" I asked.

"'Cause sometimes they aren't too smart and are mean to other animals and there are some who kill just for fun. And they kill each other lots sometimes too," one of my young nieces spoke.

"Sometimes they don't bespeck each other and us," she said again.

"That's right, sometimes they forget about respect," I said.

I continued on with the story.

"Anyway, the Ojibwe family lived up the river on a piece of land they had cleared and where they farmed hay and had a large vegetable garden. The wolves lived just back in the woods from the clearing, on the slope of the hill along a river. This family, according to my uncle, lived away from the main settlement of the Ojibwe, a male and female, and three young ones, two males and a female. And I suppose because the family chose to be isolated from their fellow Ojibwe the wolves had more opportunity to observe them, and learn of them. So they would watch them sometimes from the safety of the woods.

"My uncle shared some of the observations wolves had of the humans back then. At that time, the Ojibwe were making a rapid transition from their old ways to the ways of the new humans. Already by then, he said, many had moved away from the way they practiced their faith in the Creator and joined the new humans' religion, and although it seemed to wolves we all worship the same Creator, the new humans convinced many of the Ojibwe their old beliefs were wrong, that the Ojibwe Creator was a false god. This created conflict within the community between the ones who followed the new faith and the old, each believing their way was the only way. Also by then nearly all the Ojibwe had forsaken the animal hides they had once worn to cover their nakedness for the hides of the new humans, made from the meat of plants heretofore unknown to wolves. In a similar manner, most of the Ojibwe by that time had abandoned their round lodges and moved into the new humans' dwellings, which were made of the inner meat of trees. Many of the adults were abandoning their old language for the language of the new humans, and some of the children spoke only the new language. And, perhaps more significantly, many of the Ojibwe had forgotten the teachings of the seven grandfathers brought back to them countless generations ago by the little boy, and were instead favoring new values based on collecting things, and a preference for the needs of the individual over the group."

—

"Having an Ojibwe family the wolves could readily observe offered them much insight into the humans' ways of being. One of the observations the wolves made about this family of humans was when they engaged in play. Now, we wolves have our own ways of entertaining ourselves. As adults, we enjoy jostling and wrestling with the young, and the young engage in mock battles of dominance and submission amongst each other that will become more significant as you grow into adulthood. I know I enjoy my time with you pups when you are jumping on me, nipping at my ears and tail. In turn you do the same with each other, often until the target of the roughhousing cries out from a nip that hurts. The battle might stop for an instant, only to continue again. Sometimes your mock battles turn into real ones as one or the other will become angry. None of you, however, will be hurt. All will be quickly forgotten, forgiven.

"Now it seems the young humans engage in rough play in a similar fashion, the males especially. My uncle said the two young males in the Ojibwe family would spend much of their free time engaged in mock battles against invisible enemies, constructing and using various weapons of sticks and stones. Sometimes, the young female would be the target of their aggression. And sometimes all of them would engage in roughhousing, wrestling, just like wolves.

"Just like wolves, the human pups played a game of tag, where they would take turns running wildly and just touching the other in play. This is one of the favorite games in our wolf families. And like wolves, the human family played hide-and-go-seek.

"After darkness fell, my uncle would say, the young humans sometimes played a game they called *Windigo*, an evil cannibal, whereby two of the human pups walked across a field while one would hide and play the monster, quietly sneaking up and catching one of them, startling them with an evil growl, grabbing onto them, then pretending to eat them."

"What's a catibull, Uncle?" my niece spoke.

"Cannibals are when humans eat the flesh of other humans," I replied.

The pups said nothing, ears twitching, their dark eyes looking back at me.

"The human pups seemed to delight in frightening each other.

"Just like the humans, we wolves also acknowledge that good has a twin, an opposite. We, however, see it as part of an inner struggle in each individual, the struggle of good and the Other, of light and shadow. Each of us is capable of both.

"Unlike the humans, we don't play games involving the Other.

"Their males play a game with a stick with hide strips attached to one end and a piece of round wood, throwing the wood to each other. They work in teams, running through the woods throwing and catching the rounded wood, back and forth. And even though it is rare, every once in a while they will sound wildly when the ball is thrown between two marked trees, with a lone defender attempting to stop it from doing so.

"We play a game of tag like that too, of course. What do we use instead of a round wooden ball?"

A flurry of replies followed.

"Deer bones."

"A stick."

"A rabbit head."

I continued then.

"The wolves observed that sometimes the female pup played a game where she pretended to be a mother with a figure made of plant and animal hides in the likeness of a human newborn. And oftentimes one or both of the boys would join in, playing the role of adult male, the father.

"The adults played different games. One of them was a man's game using moccasins, the hides they wear on their feet, and sticks, a hiding game of some sort, and a hand drum made from a moose or deer hide. When they played they sang certain songs, just as we wolves do depending on the occasion."

"Do you think that humans ever watch us?" said my little niece. She continued.

"Maybe they learned to play from watching us."

"*Zhi-shay'*," she said, "do you think the humans tell stories about us wolves like we do about them?"

—

I didn't want to share with the pups that humans do observe us all the time. That sometimes they shoot wolves with a sharp thorn that has a poison that puts us to sleep. Then they put something around our necks that follows the tracks of where we go. Sometimes while we are asleep with the poison they move us to places we don't want to be, places far away from our families. That sometimes they trap wolves alive and keep them in pens so they can watch what we are doing. I would save all that for another story.

"Anyway, one time it was late morning, but the sky was already beginning to darken like night, and soon enough another family arrived at the family's home in their wagon, pulled by horses that work for the humans. The arriving family told the other family they needed to leave immediately, because there was a large fire approaching, a fire that was burning everything in sight.

"Remember when I showed you the meadow and trees not far from here where the lightning from a storm had started a fire and burned everything over a large area? Remember I told you about the smoke and heat, and how both are very dangerous to all life?"

"What's fire made from, Uncle?" asked a small voice.

"Fire is a spirit from the sun that has found its way down to *aki*. When it comes down to *aki* it can be very dangerous, very hot. It can burn everything it touches – grasses, trees, and animals, including us.

"The other humans told the family a train started the fire, the very large wagon the humans use to carry many, many people and their things; that large noisy snake that has fire coming out from it as it makes its way along the trail. Apparently some of the fire from the snake started some brush on fire, which quickly spread to the nearby woods.

"Now the wolves knew the fire was approaching long before the humans did. We have a much better sense of smell, and our eyes are much sharper. We notice things the humans have forgotten, like the meanings behind the movements of animals and birds. The wolves had seen large gatherings of birds flying away from the approaching fire, and the other animals were doing the same.

"The family of wolves could have left shortly and been far off away from the fire, but they were curious, of course, and wondered of the human family's welfare. So they watched the humans as they packed all they could into their wagon and headed off down the trail as fast as they could. Eventually they came to the Ojibwe settlement, a large clearing where other humans lived, their lodges scattered about here and there. The humans there were gathered around the largest lodge, a place they called their church. That's where they worshipped the Creator."

"Is the large lodge where the Creator lives, Uncle?" asked a voice from the huddle.

"No, it's just a place the humans gather to worship the Creator together.

"The humans quickly surmised they could not outrun the approaching fire, so they decided that everyone would go downhill to the safety of the river. It was getting darker by the minute and everyone was frightened. Even the wolves were beginning to get frightened, realizing they had observed the humans for so long they would not be able to outrun the fire as well.

"There was a male leading the humans. All the families, including the family we've been talking about, listened to the leader. He told all the females and young ones to go in the river. The males took hides and soaked them in the water and put them over the females and young ones. Soon enough, burning trees were blowing down from the top of the hill and they'd land close by where the humans were gathered. Still, the males continued to soak the hides and put them over the females and young ones so they would not burn, and they would also dunk themselves in the water so they would not catch fire.

"In the human family the wolves had been observing, the boys and father soaked their mother and sister with water as well, the father trying to reassure them they would survive. Over and over, they soaked hides and put them on the females, then dunked themselves in the water, and wore wet hides to cover themselves.

"The wolves had gone into the river as well and saw that all around them in the water were other animals who had also gone to the river for safety – bears, deer, coyotes, foxes, raccoons, lynx, horses, cattle, even dogs. The river was full of animals all the way across, and up and downstream as far as they could see. None was in fear of the other because all of their fear was for the fire. All had the common sense to run to the river to avoid the encroaching fire.

"Still, the wolves watched the humans. It was so hot their teeth hurt. And they noticed that the young humans were also curious about the fire, and how every once in a while they would lift the hides. They could see the fire all around them and felt its heat.

"Trees were flying through the air. And the wind! Fire was flying all over. Trees were blowing off the hill.

"There was a male who led the humans in prayer, a priest he was called, one of the new humans who dressed in black. He had a hide covering his body but his head was hairless and the heat was so intense that soon the top of his head was covered with blisters. He told the humans if they prayed they would not perish. To do this he held a gathering of small seeds tied together with a thin strip of hide that he used to pray, with a carving of a human on one end they say represents the Creator."

"They don't know the Creator is a wolf, do they?" said Youngest Nephew.

"The male humans continued running with wet hides and containers of water to pour on the females and young ones. The humans were screaming. They were saying to the Creator in Ojibwe, 'Help us!'

"Then they could hear other human voices coming from the top of the hill as well, speaking in their old language. Everyone, the other animals and wolves, could hear the voices.

"'Help us! Come and get us, come and help us, we're burning!'

"So the humans hollered back in Ojibwe, 'Come this way, down here by the river. Come this way.' Some of the male humans tried to go back up the hill but the fire was too hot and they retreated back to the river.

"It wasn't until the next day, after the fire had passed, that they went back up the hill to where they had heard the voices and it led them to the place where the humans buried their dead. The voices that had carried over the raging wind and fire –

"It was their dead calling to them."

——

When the pups were older and it was safe for them to travel away from camp I took them to that place along the river where the human family once lived. Now the field they once farmed is growing over with brush, and stone foundations mark where a barn and home once stood.

"These are the fields the young humans once played in," I told the pups. "Imagine you could see them now, playing tag and hide-and-go-seek, and the game they call *Windigo*. Imagine the young males and their friends playing the game with sticks and strips of hide, and a round ball of wood. Imagine the adult male playing the game with sticks and the hide that covered their feet, of the drum and their singing."

Then we walked down the old trail, now overgrown with trees, the trail the human family took to the Ojibwe settlement. The ruts of the wagons that once tread there are still worn deep into *aki*. The settlement is no longer there. Rusted metal containers, stone foundations, and several fields that once contained their dwellings are all that remain, high on a hill overlooking the river.

A newer building stands where some of the Ojibwe of today still go to worship the Creator. The original church burned in the fire, of course, as well its replacement some years later after someone was careless with an inside fire used to cook food.

"Do the Ojibwe still worship here?" a voice came from somewhere among the pups.

"Just a few nowadays, mostly the elderly. Many of the humans no longer gather to worship. Instead, they spend hours looking at their machines and collecting things. Some have gone back to worshipping the old way, a few, but not enough to affect the wellbeing of the community as a whole."

Next to the church is the place the humans have buried generations of their dead. I told them the human family in the story was probably buried there, each of them, and that if their great grandchildren were still connected to *aki* instead of their machines maybe they still walked the old trail and tended the burial place of their ancestors. I worry they are very quickly forgetting the stories.

"Don't ever walk among their dead," I told the pups. "There are spirits there. You need to respect them."

Then we went downhill to the river, crossing the trail where trains still travel, and I took them to the place where the humans and wolves and other animals went to escape the fire.

No Ojibwe or wolves died in the fire, although many of the new humans died, hundreds of them I have heard. Some went into their fields and lay, and were consumed by smoke and fire. Others sought safety in the holes in the ground they had dug to retrieve water. The fire was so intense it sucked all the air from these holes and they suffocated. Others tried to outrun the fire and drove their wagons further along the trail to a settlement down river where the new humans live. Maybe they didn't know, or forgot, that fire creates its own wind, and the fire and wind quickly overcame them.

We stood on the banks and I asked them to close their eyes and imagine what it must have been like when the Ojibwe and wolves and other animals were there in the water, with fire all around and above them. And then I told them to face the hill, and try to imagine it all, to imagine a fire so intense that even the dead called out to be saved.

"Imagine it," I said.

"If I was one of the wolves back then," said a voice somewhere in the huddle, "I *imagine* I would have never, ever stuck around to watch what would become of the human family and other Ojibwe. I would have gotten my sorry butt out of there as soon as I got my first sniff of that fire."

"Yeah, me too," said another voice.

"So, *Zhi-shay'*," said yet another voice, "what would you have done?"

It didn't take much thinking on my part.

"Me three."

The second file folder I opened contained a letter to the commissioner of Indian affairs. It was written by a mother requesting that she be allowed to keep her sons home from Pipestone Boarding School that year because she was ill and needed assistance in the home. I quickly went to the end of the letter and saw that it was signed by my great-grandmother and that her eldest son was my grandfather. A reply from the commissioner was attached, informing my great-grandmother that her sons must report to the boarding school as directed. Later, in reviewing other files, I found out that my great-grandmother died that winter in a flu epidemic that swept the reservation. I remember being overcome by a flood of emotions ranging from anger and disgust to grief. Anger and disgust for a government that believed it had the right to supervise the personal lives of the people of the nation it had possessed. Grief for a great-grandmother I had never known, someone who suddenly became more than just a tombstone in the old Catholic cemetery up the road from where I lived, but a person to whom I felt a strong emotional connection.

The impact of that powerful moment caused me to set down the file. My hands went to my face, and I wept quietly, causing discomfort to the other researchers who were sitting near me.

—Peacock, T. and Wisuri, M. (2002). *Ojibwe Waasa inaabida.*
Ojibwe We Look in All Directions.
Afton, MN: Afton Historical Society Press, p. 65-66.

CHAPTER TEN

Little Boy, Little Girl

(Love, Bravery)

"THE SPIRITS," YOUNGEST NEPHEW BEGAN. "Why did they cry out for help during the fire? I mean, they were dead, weren't they?"

"Yes, of course," I replied. "Sometimes, however, a soul-spirit will remain here on *aki* for a long while rather than making the journey straightaway to the star world. Sometimes those who have been left behind miss the dying so much, their grieving is so powerful it causes the dead to pity their loved ones and they don't complete their spirit journey. *Aki* has many such spirits, lost somewhere between this life and the one beyond. That is why it is important when someone passes, no matter how much we love or miss them, to prepare and send the dead off on their spirit journey. Death is not their end, but a new beginning."

"*Zhi-shay'*, I don't know what I will do when you leave this world. I might miss you too much," said Youngest Nephew.

"Me too," a set of pointy ears and black eyes said somewhere in the huddle.

"Me three," said another voice, giggling.

—

The next evening I called all the pups together again.

"So," I began, "are you growing tired of the humans yet?"

"Oh no, not yet," a voice somewhere in the huddle. "They can be kind of dumb sometimes but we need to know all we can about them. They are kind of in charge here on *aki*, aren't they? Or at least they think they are."

"Yeah, dumb and stupid at the same time," said the pup that enjoys saying the word 'stupid.'

"Yes, I'm afraid there are many of them who feel they are in charge. I don't know how or where that sense came from, but nevertheless, it is one of the things about them that makes them intriguing, and so dangerous at the same time."

I changed topics then.

"So tonight," I began, "I'm going to tell you about a little boy and girl and their wolf dog. It's a pretty good story. I heard it from my uncle."

"How do you remember all these stories again, Uncle?" my little niece asked.

"Because," I replied, "I have the biggest, most pointiest ears ever."

I hear everything.

—

"The boy and girl lived with their family near a meadow, a clearing in the woods in *Nagachiwanong*, the bottom of the lake, very near where we live today. As young children they walked the old trails that intersected the land with their brothers and cousins. And each spring and fall the meadow would show part of its story to them: Old stone foundations and homes of the old village that had stood there before the great fire, rusted kettles and old pottery, a cluster of trees that once served as shade and for the children of that time to climb. Even as children, it seemed each time they stood in that place it would sing to them. And they would wonder about all the stories of that place, of the people who had spent their lives there and who also reflected on its powerful presence.

"Even many years later as grandparents, they would often return and walk the old road that follows the hills that overlook the river up to that small parcel of land. In some places, the horse drawn wagons which passed through there many years ago still showed some effects, the road being worn deep into the hill. Often they would sit in the tall grass and listen to the sounds of wind, the creak of trees, and all the voices of life that celebrated that sacred place.

"They knew they belonged there. Their great-grandparents and grandparents and parents and cousins and brothers and sisters had all walked these same hills. Their bones lay buried just several hundred yards further up the river road, in the old reservation cemetery. It was the very existence of their memories that separated them from the new humans on this place we call *aki*. Their people had been here for many thousands of years. Their ancestors were part of that place, their physical existence long ago recycled into the very trees and grasses and flowers and animals that celebrated the dance of life. That is why they considered that place sacred.

"All of us have our own sacred places. Places seen through our childhood eyes. Places associated with grandmas and grandpas. When we become adults we return to them because their powerful and healing ways cause us to reflect. They offer solace and respite in difficult times. They offer us a direct pathway to the Creator, because when we are in these places we can feel the Creator's presence in every flower and leaf, every wisp of cloud and wind and smell. And if we are gone for many winters and we return to these places after a long journey, it feels like it is our grandmother who greets us. We burrow our faces deep into her fur and become buried deep into her bosom.

"*Nookomis*, grandmother, I have missed you so much, we say.

"We are honored to live in such a place."

—

"Like so many families of the day, they were poor. Four boys and a girl, their father worked in the woods as a logger, their mother stayed home to care for the family. Their home was a two-room tarpaper shack without electricity or running water, built with rough lumber from funds received by the government as a result of the great fire. And farther out in the bush, a ways upriver in a cluster of white pine surrounded by marshland, lived their mother's parents, *Nooko*, a shortened, personal name for grandmother, and *Mishoomis*, their grandfather. The boys and girl spent much time there as well, for their grandparents' wigwam, covered with boards and tarpaper, was as much home for the children as that of their parents.

"The woods and river were their playgrounds. They fished in spring, summer, and fall, mostly for catfish and bullheads, then cleaned them and sold them to neighbors. Some, always, were skinned and brought home to feed the family. They hunted squirrels and partridge, and in winter set snares for rabbits, which were sold or brought home for food. They picked and sold berries of all colors and varieties, and their mother made jams and jellies with some of it. Any money made was handed over to their mother to buy necessities. Their father and grandfather occasionally brought home deer, and their mother and grandmother prepared the hides, which were made into moccasins and sold to the occasional tourists. The parents and grandparents all harvested wild rice each fall, selling most to a buyer, but finishing some for home use. And although they all knew how to speak the new humans' English, they rarely conversed in it except during the rare trips to town, where they interacted with the new ones. At night, their home lit by kerosene lamps, and depending on the season heated with an old kitchen wood stove, they spoke the language of their ancestors, the sing-song cadence echoing off the walls and out through the cold air.

"Sometimes in the cold winter evenings when they could afford batteries they would all gather round the radio and listen to the music of the day, the big band sound, swing.

"The boy and girl were the oldest of the children, ages ten and seven respectively. Neither had yet seen the inside of a school. Few reservation children attended the new humans' local school in the town just downriver, as the government agent sent most off to the schools established for the

Indians, as they called the Ojibwe. Late every summer he would appear at the doors of the families of the reservation with his list, along with a large man from another tribe, who spoke a language they were unfamiliar with, who would be the one who would transport them off several days south and west to the Indian school.

"They had no choice to defy the agent when he came for the children, for although they were able to gather much of the sustenance they needed from the land through harvest, hunting, and fishing, they were still reliant on the government for flour, potatoes, and salt pork. Without these rations there would not be enough food to go around. The parents and grandparents had all lived through starving times, without rations, when the land was still barren from the killing off of the animals after the days of the fur trade.

"*Zhi-shay',*" a voice said from somewhere in the huddle, "is that when we wolves were nearly hunted to extinction?"

"Yes," I replied. "These were difficult times. This is a difficult story for me to tell because of what happened to the young ones back then. They were just pups, like you. Do you want me to tell another story?"

"No," a reply from somewhere in the huddle of ears, fur, and tails.

"Some of the stories make me sad, Uncle," said another voice.

"I know, I'm so sorry. I promise to make you laugh when this is all over with, okay?" I replied.

"I think that agent was stupid," said the one who liked using the word 'stupid.'

"I think what he did on behalf of his government was wrong," I replied.

"Anyway, the agent and the man from another tribe appeared at the home of the boy and girl one day in late summer and told their parents they had come for them, the boy, the girl.

"'Are you the mother of Samuel, age ten, and Rebecca, age seven?' the agent asked.

"And as the mother stood there looking through the unopened screen door staring at the agent and the man from another tribe, she wanted to say to them:

"'We call them Samuel and Rebecca only because the priest who works with you insisted on their baptism in the church, saying they needed Bible names. We don't call them by those names here in our home. These may be the names you call them by, but my boy here, his name is *Giniw*, Golden Eagle, and the girl, *Wabigwannce*, Little Flower. These are the names our Creator knows them by. These are the names my father, their grandfather, dreamed for them.'

"But she didn't say what she wanted to say. She stood there, strong, biting her lip.

"'Next week,' he said, 'we'll come by. Make sure they are ready. There's no need to pack. They'll be issued clothing once they get there.'

"'Where will you be taking them?' their mother asked, speaking in her broken English singsong cadence, voice shaking, heart near broken.

"'Pipestone Indian School.'

"On the day the agent and the man from another tribe came to get the boy and girl, the family was there to send them on their way. Their mother had made them bannock, pan bread, to nibble on during their journey, wrapping it in cloth. Their father made each a necklace of soft deerskin, on them a small bundle containing parts of an eagle bone, feather, and small stones from the river. Their little brothers, both too young to remember that day, stood clinging to their mother's dress. Their grandparents held hands with the boy and girl as they walked to the waiting government bus.

"'*Gigawaabamin, menawa,*' all said, nearly at the same time. I will see you later.

"'*Mashkawisen,*' their grandfather said. Be strong.

"'*Zaugin,*' all said. I love you.

"They found their way to an empty seat and each pressed their faces against the window glass, Samuel and Rebecca holding hands, each of their faces contorted in fear and pain.

"And as the bus disappeared down the trail, both the grandmother and mother could be heard.

"Wailing softly."

—

"The parents had heard the stories about these schools from those who had returned from them after many years. Some spoke of the beatings for speaking their language. Others showed the damage from abuse in all its forms, of matrons, teachers, and administrators leading small children off to their quarters late in the evenings. For those who had suffered such horrific treatment not even drink could soften the pain, the nightmares.

"Neither Samuel nor Rebecca suffered from beatings or emotional or sexual abuse. Each was careful to confine the speaking of their language with other Ojibwe to late in the evenings when most everyone was asleep, or when they found themselves together without others around in the laundry or outside, or while washing dishes, or cleaning.

"School was not beatings or abuse – it was loneliness."

"*Zhi-shay'*, why did they send Samuel and Rebecca to that school?" It was my young niece.

So I tried to explain why the new humans' government forced the Ojibwe and other tribes' children off to boarding schools.

"The schools were all over Ojibwe country, and everywhere else throughout the land controlled by the new humans. There, the males were trained in farming or manual labor, the females to be domestics, to work in the homes of the new humans, or to be homemakers. All of the schools sought to cleanse the young ones of any connections to their parents, community, and tribe. Many of the young were removed from their parents for years, and thus removed from their ways of being, their culture and spiritual teachings, with the stated purpose of removing all things Ojibwe about them, to make them new humans.

"The new humans' government required these children to attend boarding schools, a rule that was enforced by threat of withholding rations. In some instances, the agents took the children by force, as young as four human winters. This continued on for generations.

"At many of the schools the children would spend an equal amount of time in classroom and doing labor. The new humans' government did not direct a lot of effort to ensure these schools had all they needed, and thus exploited the labor of the children in order to operate.

"At Pipestone, Samuel and Rebecca met many children from other tribes, including the Dakota, Oneida, Pottawatomie, Arikara, and Sac and Meskwakwi. Each day there followed a routine. Children were awakened early at sunrise to the sound of a bugle, made of a shiny metal, sounding familiar like the call of a goose. They were marched here and there, according to a strict schedule of making beds, brushing teeth, breakfast, and assigned manual work. Then school, where they learned the new humans' spoken and written tongue, new ways of knowing the earth and sky, of counting. Then more school and doing manual work. Supper. Before they were sent to their dormitories they were given a short period of free play. This is the only time that Samuel and Rebecca got to visit during their time at the school. Then they were marched to their sleeping quarters. The bugle announced bedtime.

"Several days a week they were marched to the new human's church, where they were told their old spiritual teachings were the words of a devil, an evil one. They were also told the Creator had a son named Jesus who died for their wrongs, and they learned to pray to Him; his likeness hung from a wooden cross on the wall.

"Earlier I mentioned that neither Samuel nor Rebecca suffered punishment or abuse there, but that does not mean they were not witness to it against others. Runaways, once caught, were beaten, then locked away alone in a room for days and fed stale bread and water. Girls were forced to wear boys' clothes and boy's the girls' dresses as punishment for misbehavior. Some had all of their hair shaved for not following the rules, or for perceived insolence or rebelliousness. Talking back or swearing, even speaking their language was met by forcing lye soap into their mouths. The soap was strong enough to burn the insides. Diseases spread rampantly in the schools, and many died. Samuel and Rebecca each had friends that became ill and died from a host of diseases. Others died while running away, from freezing to death, starvation, getting hit by trains.

An untold number died of loneliness.

"While there, Samuel and Rebecca worked in all manner of labor, depending on whether it was considered male or female work. On a given day they could be found in the kitchen, barns, gardens, washing dishes, tables, and floors, ironing, sewing, darning, and doing carpentry.

"Neither received any word from their parents while there. Their parents were considered illiterate, not trained in the new humans' written language. Nor was either allowed to go home in spring. They were sent together to work on a local farm, where they spent the summers.

"They met *Makwa* (Bear) there.

"*Makwa* was the product of a union of a male wolf and a large black female dog, a Newfoundland. He had lived nearly the entirety of his young life chained to a post in the farmyard."

"What's a new found dog?" asked a voice from somewhere in the huddle.

"A big one, bigger than wolves. Black." My response.

—

"The farmer and his wife treated them well enough. Samuel worked hard with the man, milking, feeding the horses and cows, mucking the barn, picking rocks from the field, learning to fix equipment that was constantly in need of repair. Rebecca spent most of her time with the woman, scrubbing unfinished wood floors with a brush on her hands and knees, gardening, weeding, feeding chickens and gathering eggs, harvesting, canning, cooking, and doing dishes. Each night they went to bed exhausted, only to arise before sunrise and do the same over again, day after day, week after week for months.

"And during the rare moments they had unscheduled time they would meet up in the yard and visit with each other and Bear, as the farmer and his wife knew him by. There they would talk softly in the language, and soon enough Bear began to understand it as well. They could not fathom why the farmer and his wife would keep the wolf dog chained to a post.

Bear had lived that way since he was a few months old.

"Samuel and Rebecca were chained in their own way."

———

"They did this for two winters, Samuel now twelve, Rebecca nine.

"'I can't do this anymore, brother. I miss our parents, grandmother, grandfather, the river. I want to go home,' Rebecca cried softly one day as they talked together in the farmyard, all the while petting Bear, scratching his ears and belly until one of his rear legs jerked uncontrollably in a scratching motion in the air at nothing. It was late summer and they would soon be returning to the school.

"So a plan was hastily put into place. They would hoard what food they could, warm clothing, a blanket, a knife.

"'We'll walk the trails, the railroad tracks at night. Home is north. We know the stars. Bear will come with us. In evening he'll keep us warm, protect us.'

"They gathered together what they could for several weeks. Hid it backside of the chicken coop, where it lay covered with a tarp and timbers.

"And one night they put their plan in motion, snuck quietly from their rooms and met out in the farmyard near Bear. They unchained him, and when they did he was so overjoyed he knocked Samuel over, standing over him, licking his face.

"'*Makwa, bizaan daga,*' whispered Samuel. Bear, quiet please.

"Then in the blackness of night they were off."

———

"They walked north through the evening and those that followed, using the stars, hiding in the ditches whenever one of the new humans and their machines would happen by. They drank water from the occasional stream, filling a container for later use. They shared a can of beans, some dried meat, each of them getting small portions: Samuel, Rebecca, Bear. They slept during daylight, cuddled closely together, heads burrowed deeply into Bear's soft fur, hiding among the trees and fields should the man from another tribe happen by in search of them. And although they knew it went against their teachings, hunger drove them to raid farms of produce, eggs and an occasional chicken, which they cooked and ate greedily, always sharing, always ensuring the other got enough to sustain themselves.

"They all knew, however, that their walking alone would never take them home. There had to be another way.

"'I know there is a train that makes its way north and east,' Rebecca said. 'I seen it in a book.'

"So they found the railroad trail and headed north and east in search of the snake that breathes fire, in search of one that was stopped as it was being loaded with this or that with the new humans' things, with coal, cattle.

"And one day they found such a train.

"They waited until evening, until the humans who guarded the snake were asleep or careless. Then they found an empty car. Bear was lifted up first. He was the heaviest of them all and it took both Samuel and Rebecca to do it. Then Rebecca. Samuel climbed in last. He closed the door just enough to hide them, and they waited until late the next day and well into the evening until the snake gave a jerk, and the whoosh of its engine started it on its journey.

"They moved slowly north and east for a day or more. Then late in the evening they came to a steep hill, the sacred mountain of their people, and below was the waters of the big lake glimmering in the moonlight, the lake that bears the likeness of the wolf. And across the bay the snake stopped and they climbed down and ran, hiding in the woods.

"Samuel knew that home was just several days walk to the south and west. Again they walked in the darkness of night, hiding during the day, following the river, the river that led home.

"Then late in the evening of the second day of walking south and west, they finally made it home, climbing the hill to the meadow, and there, in the clearing through their home's only window was the soft glow of a kerosene lamp, turned low to signify the occupants were long in bed.

"A quiet tap on the window.

"*'Nimama. Indayday,'* they both said at the same time, my mother, my father.

"And their mother, who knew the voices of her children as only a mother would know because she had known them long before they were born, to when each lay curled deep inside her, arose and opened the door."

—

"The next day Samuel and Rebecca's mother and father hid them in the woods should the agent or man from another tribe come looking for them to return them to that place. In darkness they headed north up the old trail that followed the ridgeline of the hills overlooking the river, up into the deep bush, to their grandparent's wigwam. For neither the agent nor the man from another tribe would ever think to search for them there."

"*Zhi-shay*'," it was my young niece. "Whatever happened to Samuel, Rebecca, Bear?"

"Bear lived with the grandparents until he was fat and old. He helped haul their firewood on a sled in winter, and always slept between the door and woodstove and was their protector. He learned to understand the language fluently.

"Samuel and Rebecca stayed with the grandparents as well, until the agent and man from another tribe grew tired of coming to the parents' home in search of them. Then when they were older, Samuel sixteen, Rebecca thirteen, they returned home to live with their parents.

"As an adult Samuel worked in the new humans' wood mill, where they ground the meat of trees into powder and made things from it. And later as an old man he became the bingo caller at the tribe's casino. The dust from years of working in the mill claimed him though, poisoned his lungs. I'll take you to where he is buried if you'd like. He chose to be buried where he was born, near the old stone foundation of the home that once stood there in the meadow.

"Rebecca became a nurse's aide at the reservation hospital, and later at the community clinic, working with the sick and injured. She's grown to be very old.

"I saw them both together several years ago, before Samuel's passing. Samuel and Rebecca were walking the railroad tracks upriver, and when they reached a certain place they climbed the hill to the meadow, to the place that was long ago a village where the people lived. When they reached the foundation of their old home they sat in the grass and talked and laughed softly in the language. They shared a sandwich of government spam and homemade bread, and took turns drinking from a jug of Kool Aid."

"*Zhi-shay*,'" it was Youngest Nephew. "You said Rebecca has grown to be very old. That means she is still alive. Am I right?"

"Could we see her?" asked my young niece.

So one night when the pups were older and it was safe for them to travel we made our way a bit downriver and across several fields to a lodge where many of the elderly of the village now reside. There we gathered outside the window of her apartment, a huddle of fur, ears and tails, and watched her as she sat rocking in her chair, watching the machine the humans spend so much time staring at.

Then we headed on home, and when we got there I gathered them together again.

"So, I promised to end the story with something funny. How about this one?

"What did the humans say when they saw a pack of wolves coming over a hill with sunglasses on?

"Nothing. They didn't recognize them."

—

"That's stupid, Uncle," said Stupid, I mean the one who always says the word 'stupid.'

"What was that thing, sunglasses?"

One year we buried eight of my friends and relatives, including my sister. Most were lost to alcohol and cars slamming into trees. What lessons can we learn from their deaths? I know I have buried too many of my loved ones over the years. There are no lessons in that.

—Peacock, T. and Wisuri, M. (2002). *The Good Path*. Afton, MN: Afton Historical Society Press, p. 100.

CHAPTER ELEVEN

The Time of the Sixth Fire

(Honesty, Bravery, Love)

SEVERAL EVENINGS LATER WE GATHERED together again to talk story. I was hoping the pups had had time to reflect on the story I had told them about Samuel and Rebecca, and they did.

"Uncle," it was my young niece. "How did your uncle learn the story of Samuel and Rebecca?"

"Our aunties and uncles before my uncle, going several generations back, heard it from a wolf who knew Bear. Remember, Bear had a wolf side. Bear went deep into the bush every now and then, and on one of those occasions he befriended a lone wolf, one in search of a new family. He approached the wolf submissively, as he should. They became friends and would talk story. Bear shared the story of his journey from the farm-yard to living with the elders, of Samuel and Rebecca. And when the wolf found a new home among other wolves he shared the story with them. Several generations of wolves followed the lives of Samuel and Rebecca as they grew into adulthood, became elders."

"I think that Samuel and Rebecca saved Bear when they freed him. I think if they hadn't done that he would have died chained up like that," said a voice somewhere in the huddle.

"You're right," I replied. "The boy and girl could have just left him there. We all have the potential to do that, ignore the suffering of others. At the same time we have the ability to unchain. That's our choice. Bear, once freed, was an asset to the boy and girl. He protected them on their journey home, kept them warm at night. And once he found a home with the grandparents he protected the elders as well.

"There are so many lessons in the story of Samuel and Rebecca," I continued. "It just as well could have ended much differently. Many of the young ones who ran away from those schools never made it home. The man from another tribe caught most of them. Others turned themselves in because they became lost, were cold and tired, starving. Some died along the way. But the little boy and girl made it home. They got to live out their lives until they were old. They got to share their story of survival with their family, and when they were older there were people who came to them with machines that captured their images and voices and saved it so others could hear their story. The people who saved their story also scratched Samuel and Rebecca's words onto the thing they call paper which humans decipher, so their words will live on for a long time, maybe forever.

"They were brave, that little boy and girl. All the generations of young ones following them can find lessons in their story."

—

"Now tonight's story, okay?" I said.

"Go for it, Uncle," said a voice somewhere in the huddle. I think it was Stupid, I mean the one who always says the word 'stupid.'

"Remember many nights ago we talked about the prophecies, the fires? I want to return to that sixth fire because that is where the humans find themselves now, somewhere along the trail of the sixth and the beginning of the seventh fire. Again, I need to remind you that wolves and humans are parallel beings; what happens to one will happen to the other. So we wolves also find ourselves somewhere in both the sixth and seventh fires at the same time. When I tell you about the humans, I want you to think about how their story applies to us, to wolves. When you imagine the humans in the story, replace them with us, with wolves. In turn, we would hope the humans do the same."

"But we aren't suffering like they are," my young niece said. "At least not as much."

"Maybe you're right," I replied. "We have suffered greatly, however, and will again, but you're right in a way. They, the humans, have changed so much since the coming of the new humans.

"We, however, are still wolves.

"This all started," I began again, "when the new humans arrived. Now I'm not blaming what happened to the Ojibwe and other tribes on the new humans. It's just that a set of circumstances all came together at the same time and set off a chain of events that in the end led to this prolonged period of suffering we are confronted with today.

"First it was the diseases they brought that killed off many tribes, and in other places claimed most of the young and elderly. Then wars. Wars in which the new humans' sticks that breathe fire were vastly superior to the tribes' bows and arrows and spears. In the process, the new humans took their lands, their livelihoods. They confined them to land that was useless for harvesting either meat or growing crops. With no food, the ones who remained became dependent on the new humans' rations, and even more subjected to the new humans' will. Then they took their children to the boarding schools, where they sought to remove all things Ojibwe or Dakota or whatever tribe they were, to make them new humans."

"That's also when wolves were nearly exterminated," said a voice somewhere in the huddle.

"That's right," I replied.

"All of this took a difficult toll on the tribes' sense of wellbeing, their ability to deal with all the things that were happening to them. In the process it damaged their immune system, their ability to fight off all the bad things happening to them, and their psyche, their inner self, their soul-spirit. So all of these bad things that happened to them hurt all the way to their souls.

"And it didn't end with that. Some of the adults turned to drink to drown their pain. Some took their own lives. Others became angry, took the lives of others, or became victims of another's rage. Some took it out on others through all manner of abuse. Whether you are drowning from a bottle, or in many feet of water, it doesn't matter. Suffering is suffering. You cannot say one is more than the other. What matters is that sometimes the pain is so bad it damages all the way to the soul."

"*Zhi-shay*," it was Youngest Nephew, "I think that if Samuel and Rebecca had not made it home, if they had died on their journey, it would have damaged the souls of their parents and grandparents. And if Bear would have had to live his life chained to a post in the farmyard, his soul would have been damaged."

My nephew, sometimes when he says things it nearly takes my breath away. I just sat there for a while contemplating what he had just said, digesting the fact that he gets it. He gets it and maybe some of the others do as well.

My hesitation got the attention of one of the pups, of course.

"Uncle," said a voice from somewhere in the huddle, "Did you forget the story?"

—

"I want to return for a bit to what your sister, my niece, had to say just a few moments ago, how sometimes some of us are able to recover when horrible things happen.

"Why is it the humans continue to suffer so deeply while we wolves have seemingly recovered? We, after all, were nearly hunted to extinction because of the new humans' fear of wolves. We were trapped for our furs, or because some of us found the animals they kept quite tasty and they blamed all wolves for the actions of a few.

"The difference, possibly, is that wolves remained wolves. The things that hold us together as a group, our culture, remained strong. The way we govern, the alpha male and female, beta, mid-level, even the omega. None of that changed. We hunt as a group. Some go for the flank, some for the underbelly, for the snout. That hasn't changed. Perhaps most important, our values remain strong. We haven't forgotten the lessons of the grandfathers from the star world brought down to *aki* by the little boy. We haven't forgotten that the answer to all the troubles we encounter is in *zagaa'idiwin*, love. We care for our young, respect our elders, we live our lives to their fullest, we mourn our dead in a good way. None of that has changed.

"We are still wolves.

"For the Ojibwe and other tribal humans, however, the suffering has continued for generations and nearly destroyed them. The way they raised their children was warped by boarding schools. Their spiritual practices were maligned and outlawed by the new humans' priests and missionaries, and this tore away what held them together as a community. Their old ways of leading, once defined by their moral teachings and clan system, were replaced by a system modeled after the new humans' way of leading, based on power, where a few have it and compete with others for it. War and diseases not only claimed many of them, it took their healers as well. Nothing escaped the carnage. Some replaced the love they had in their hearts for the Creator and others with a love of possessions, the needs of the group with their own needs.

"Their wounds have passed down from generation to generation. The deep pain they experienced, the soul wound, has passed down from grandparent to parent, parent to child. When the child becomes adult they pass it down to their children. This goes on and on and still there has been no end.

"And in the end, what made them Ojibwe or Dakota or whatever tribe they are has been compromised.

"With wolves, our culture continues to function well enough, and because of it many of the bad things that have happened to us haven't had such a devastating effect. The Ojibwe and other tribes suffered the loss of their histories, stories, languages, and belief systems, all the things that make up their culture.

"If we could talk to them we might ask them: Tell me your history, your stories, speak to me in your language. Show how you live your belief systems. Tell me all the stories about the Ojibwe sky. Most, I'm afraid, might be able to tell us a little about who they are, what makes them Ojibwe. Maybe they will say they are 'Indian' or 'Chippewa,' but these names are the new humans' descriptions for them. Maybe they will know about their cultural hero, First Human, *Waynabozho*, but most will not. Most will be able to recite only stories they have learned about in the new humans' schools, of George Washington, fairies and elves, or the goose that laid the golden egg. Maybe they will be able to say something in their old language, *makwa* or *beshig*, bear or one, but most will be fluent only in the new humans' English. If we were to ask them about the teachings of the seven grandfathers, most will know nothing of the story. They will, however, be able to tell you, if you ask, about the things they possess, the positions they hold that signify their self-importance, their machines, the teams they watch on the machines that cause them to cheer loudly.

"There are whole groups of them who know nothing about being Ojibwe. They have no interest in the ways of their ancestors, it's the past they say and we can only move forward. Even though they may be members of the tribe and reap its benefits – health care, schooling, housing, work on the reservation, and so on. They are never seen at summer pow-wows or other community gatherings, or at ceremonies. They may or may not identify with being Ojibwe.

"Most will not be able to tell their creation story, or the naming of *aki* by First Human and wolf. Some even display the hides of wolves on their walls and say that is their culture.

"And really, it's not their fault because all of that was stripped from them, because none of that is as important as knowing and living the values of what really defines being Ojibwe – wisdom, love, respect, bravery, honesty, humility, and truth."

"Especially love," my little niece. "That's what ties all the values together."

Sometimes I think the pups know more than I do, my niece especially. "That's right," I said.

"And when all of that happens," I continued on, "we see a breakdown, when the things that held the people together as one fall apart into little pieces, drift away, disappear."

"But there are still Ojibwe who live the values, aren't there?" Youngest Nephew asked.

"Of course there are, many, but not enough to turn things around. And they are being bombarded everyday by their machines to possess more, take more for themselves."

"Why can't they just get over it? Didn't we get over what happened to us?" asked another voice somewhere in the huddle.

"The difference," I replied, "is that when the hunters and trappers came and slaughtered as they did, a small core of our ancestors hid deep in the bush where they couldn't be found. Those few were able to use their sight, hearing, smell, speed, and hunting ability to run, hide, and survive. And once the killing time was over they remained wary of humans, avoiding them as we still do. Only because of these unique skills are we still here.

"Wolves.

"The Ojibwe had nowhere to hide."

—

"*Zhi-shay'*," Youngest Nephew spoke. "You said when all of those bad things happened there was a breakdown, when the things that held the people together fell apart into little pieces.

"What does that look like?"

—

"When I was a pup one of my aunties, *Ogichidaquay* (Woman Warrior), took us in close to their villages to see what it looked like because I had the same question. Along the way we came upon a human who lay as in death on the side of the road.

"'Is the human dead, Auntie?' I remember asking.

"'*Gaween*, no, but his spirit is broken,' she answered, 'and I suppose that is like a kind of death, to be alive but to have somehow lost your spirit.'

"So I asked what was wrong with him and Auntie told me the human was *giwashkwaybi*, drunk.

"'What is this thing, drunk?' I asked.

"And she told me about how sometimes in late summer when the berries and apples become overripe that little creatures too small to see enter them and change them in a way that the fruit, when consumed, causes whoever eats them to become drunk. These changed fruit slur the speech, she said, like if we try to talk with too much water or food in our mouths. Drink causes clumsiness because it delays the messages sent from our head to the muscles in our body, causes stomach pains, vomiting, nausea.

"The humans make a liquid from the berries. Sometimes they drink so much it leads to a loss of consciousness or blacking out, so when they wake up they don't remember periods of when they were drinking. And if they drink for days, weeks, months, or years, their faces will get a redness and puffiness. In the end their bodies might even shut down, and the thing inside them that cleans the blood will shut down, killing them."

"Yaaaaay, said a voice somewhere in the huddle. "Let's go berry hunting."

He was teasing of course.

"So, do wolves ever get drunk?"

"Certainly, but not on purpose. Sometimes wolves will eat the fruit that will make them drunk. Our distant relatives, the coyotes, are known to climb right into the apple trees in the fall and eat the fruit, which is sometimes changed, so they seem to become drunk more than we do," I replied.

Then again," I continued, "coyotes don't have much common sense anyway."

"*Zhi-shay'*," said another voice from the huddle, "have you ever been drunk?"

"I think so," I said. "A long time ago I ate some blueberries that made me slur my talk, feel dizzy. I remember I went to nap and when I awoke my head hurt like a bear had sat on it all night."

"But I don't understand," it was my young niece, "what does getting drunk have to do with someone who has a broken spirit?"

"Some of the humans drink too much, too often. The changed fruit helps them forget their pain," I replied. "It softens the hurt, if only for a while.

"The human who lay on the side of the road," I continued, "we can only pity him. We can only imagine his pain. And at the same time we must pity all those whom he loves and love him in return, because they also bear the weight of his pain, the pain he causes by his drinking, the things he says and does when he's drunk.

"Drink, however, isn't the only thing we see when things break down into little pieces, drift away, disappear."

"Can you show us, Uncle?" It was Youngest Nephew. "Like Auntie *Ogichidaquay* did for you? Maybe if we see it we will understand better this thing, breaking down."

So when the pups were a bit older and it was safe for them to travel, we made several trips near the villages of the humans, and along the way and while there I talked story and showed them what the pieces of things broken looked like, the poverty, both physical and that of the spirit. Of the health problems, of growing fat from eating too many starchy foods, of using food to soften the pain, of high blood pressure, diabetes, heart disease, of mental health problems, especially chronic depression. Of unresolved grief from seeing too many loved ones die, of heroin and methamphetamine and oxycodone, crack cocaine, of gangs, of people who can't find jobs, or hold jobs, or were in jobs that couldn't support them. Of little girls becoming pregnant, of mistrust, of a loss of faith in self, others, the tribe, the Creator itself. Of crime, accidents and the injuries and deaths that went along with these things, of children being raised without a father, mother, of abuse in all its forms.

Of a sense of helplessness, a feeling that there is no way out and that no one cares, of perfect pain. Of self hate, of identifying with all the suffering of their ancestors and developing a victim identity.

"Uncle." It was my little niece. "All of this seems so big, like maybe this has gone on for too long and they have gotten too far off the trail. Maybe it is too late for them."

"Remember," I said, "what I have told you, shown you, is not inside everyone. Just enough to make their villages be out of balance. And there are many others who were lost along the trail and have found their way on the path again. When they do, when they have genuine healing, it makes them more compassionate, more caring for others. Picking up the pieces begins with the individual, one at a time, then a few more, then a community, a tribe, a nation.

"You know, my niece, you understand because you've reminded us all before where the answers lie to these questions. The ones who have healed, the ones who then work to heal others, the groups who support each other in their healing, all of this is circular of course.

"The Creator is the same for them and us. We do not ask the Creator, 'Give me peace. Give me hope. Heal my pain.'"

"The Creator is peace, hope," she replied. "And love is the healing."

And when she said that it took my breath away.

My niece. She gets it.

She gets it.

———

"Uncle, you're being quiet for a long time. Did you eat them berries?"

There were once an estimated two or more million wolves in North America before they were hunted, trapped and poisoned to near extermination. Today there are less than 80,000 remaining (60,000 in Canada, 18,000 in the United States). Most of the wolves in the United States are in the states of Alaska (12,000), Minnesota (2,700), Wisconsin (750), Michigan (750) and the western states of Idaho, Montana and Wyoming (1,700).

—Wikipedia contributors, "List of gray wolf populations by country,"
Wikipedia, The Free Encyclopedia.

CHAPTER TWELVE

When We Were Hunted

(Love, Honesty, Humility)

THE PUPS, OF COURSE, HAD their opinions about the humans after I told them the story of the Sixth Fire, and several evenings later when we gathered together to talk story I heard about it.

"They're messed up, aren't they, Uncle?"

"Yeah, a lot of them don't even know what it means to be Ojibwe anymore. We're still wolves. We haven't forgotten who we are."

"We ain't eating them berries all the time either like some of them do either."

To which one of the pups lay on its back with its legs up in the air, tail also standing tall tucked firmly between its legs, eyes closed tightly, still.

"I been eating the berries. Look at me!"

All the while they were also just being pups, laughing, chasing each other and their tails, nipping and biting, wrestling.

When I was finally able to gather them all together, and relative quiet set in among them, it was Stupid, I mean the one who always says the word 'stupid,' who opened up the evening's topic.

"So, what kind of stupid things are they going to do now?"

—

"Tonight you'll learn about when we were nearly hunted to extermination. I asked your Auntie if she would tell it to you. She knows the story better than I do. Auntie Ona?"

Auntie *Onoshenyan,* their mother's sister, stepped forward.

Her voice was soft and low, sweet, in the singsong manner of the aunties. Even those who had trouble settling down became still, as well those who often spent story time nipping at others' tails, who I often had to tell to be still, became quiet. For no one, including me, would ever dare cross an auntie. She stood before them for what seemed like the longest time, looking them up and down, silently. It got so quiet the only sounds were of wolf pups breathing.

She gave them that look.

Then she talked story.

"The new humans feared and hated wolves long before they came across the ocean to this land. In their old lands, wolves had already been killed to near extinction. So when they came here they continued what they began there, only on a more massive scale, and at the same time they were also killing the buffalo, deer, caribou, elk, moose, and tribes of humans who lived here at the same time. Maybe their fear of wolves came from the fact they heard us howling, but rarely saw us. And when they did see us, we ran from them, for our fear of them was as deep, or deeper, than their fear of us.

"The cattle, horses, sheep, and pigs they brought over from across the ocean were easy prey to us. These are animals that have been living among the humans for so long they have forgotten what it is like to take care of themselves. Their meat is good, so tasty."

"You're making us hungry, Auntie," said a voice from somewhere in the huddle.

"I like pig the best," a pup whispered to the one next to him.

The look.

"Sorry Auntie."

She continued.

"So when our wolf ancestors took some of their livestock for food, they fought back, combining the fear they had of us from their stories, stories of wolves as demons, of big bad wolves, of werewolves, half-human, half wolf, of wolves who stole and ate their children. All untrue, but it didn't matter. They took that fear and combined it with the fact they were losing some livestock and used it as an excuse to begin the mass extermination of our ancestors.

"At first it was the ranchers, farmers, and landowners who killed by baiting and trapping wolves. Sometimes they would dig pits and bait them, drawing in a hungry wolf. Sometimes they used the metal traps. It became somewhat a sport, to trap wolves, then set their dogs on them, who would then rip the wolves to pieces."

"I hate dogs," said a voice from somewhere in the huddle.

Auntie Ona ignored the pup and continued, "At other times the new humans would kill a deer or caribou, or another animal, and poison it with strychnine, so when wolves ate the carcass they suffered death by poison. Strychnine is made from the seeds of a kind of tree that grows in other lands, not here. The poison not only killed wolves but the other animals who fed on the carcass – eagles, crows, foxes, bears, coyotes, mice.

"So as the new humans were killing off the herd animals that wolves fed upon, at the same time wolves were feeding on some of their livestock. Farmers hired men whose only job was to trap, poison, and hunt wolves, many times using dogs. Pups were dug out of their dens and killed. These hunters were paid a bounty, a paper they used for the trade of food and other possessions.

"Even the new humans' government, their leaders, became involved in the extermination. They assigned the killing of wolves to a small group of humans who worked in their government, and these humans oversaw the killing of most of the wolves under their rule. Soon enough there were just a few wolves left, in places they call Minnesota and Michigan."

"Where is this Minnesota and Michigan?" asked a voice from somewhere in the huddle.

She looked around where they were all sitting.

"Right here, this is what they call Minnesota," she replied.

"We are the few who are left," she said.

"There are just a few of us left?" asked a voice from somewhere in the huddle.

"Auntie, could I sit up closer to you?" asked another voice from the huddle.

"Me too, Auntie?" A chorus of more voices joined in.

"Come here, all of you," she said softly.

All the pups gathered in close to her. I watched them from a distance, their Auntie soothing them, assuring they were protected, loved. Several pups burrowed their faces deep into her fur as they listened to her talk story.

"The new humans are bad, aren't they Auntie Ona?" asked Youngest Nephew.

She began licking his face and ears then, hesitating for what seemed like the longest time. Then she moved on to another pup, then another, even the one who always says the word 'stupid,' for he was the one who was closest to her, the one burrowed the deepest into her fur with his snout. Then she answered.

"No, they aren't bad. It wasn't all of them who did this, only a few. Only those who believed all the bad stories they heard about us. Many of them try to live their values. Their teachings on how to live their lives in balance are a lot like ours. Theirs were scratched onto rocks using different words. They call their seven grandfathers, angels; their teachings, commandments. They scratched on paper, this thing made from the meat of trees, the whole story of the Creator's lessons and how humans should live their lives, what they call a Bible.

"No, they aren't bad, little nieces and nephews," she said.

"They're just human."

—

"Do the new humans still kill wolves?" asked my youngest niece.

Auntie Ona turned to me with the question. I guess that meant it was my turn to come up with an answer.

"Sometimes they do when they say there are too many of us, and sometimes they don't when they say our numbers are low. I don't know what they mean by that. Their government makes these decisions, I have heard. I just know whenever they decide to have their wolf hunts they use the sticks that breathe fire as well as traps," I told them.

"But how can there be too many of us when we are all that are left?" asked a voice from somewhere in the huddle.

"What is it like to die from the sticks that breathe fire, Uncle?" asked another voice.

"What is it like to die from the traps?"

"Does that mean we are too many, us pups?" another pup asked. "Will they come for us?"

I looked over to Auntie Ona, silently asking her how I might respond to their questions. I didn't know the answers to their questions, and was sure neither did she. I had never run from the sticks that breathed fire, had never been caught in the traps. I didn't know how many of us were too many.

"I don't know," I finally responded. "Auntie Ona, do you have anything to add that helps answer their questions?"

"I don't know either," she answered.

Still, the pups asked questions of things in which we had no answers, ending with,

"Do the Ojibwe hunt us as well?"

—

The young wolves were allowed to join the hunt in the fall and their added numbers, six in all, made for more successful deer harvests, as they nearly doubled the number of hunters. And they were excellent hunters by all accounts, fast, sure, with keen noses, sight. Each was hungry to prove themselves worthy to the adults, to their parents, aunties, uncles. By this time they were nearly full-grown wolves. And the decisions on their positions within the pack, the jockeying for who would be this or that, the future alpha and beta male and female, the warriors, mid-levels, and omega were being played out, determined. The struggles for dominance can be hard during this time; while often more posturing than anything else, it still left more than its share of bloodied competitors, injuries. The ways of wolves sometimes may seem harsh to an outsider looking in, but it is how we have survived for countless millennia, still wolves. And as their uncle, I could only stand back and let what happened, happen. The pup who always said the word stupid, as well my youngest nephew and niece, rose above all others during this time. I always knew they would.

We had heard from our watchers, the wolves who continually followed the movements and actions of the Ojibwe, that the new humans would be having a wolf hunt that fall. The watchers sometimes looked to the machines the humans stared at so much, but only from the safety of the tree line and through the openings the humans have in their dwellings.

"One of their leaders," the watcher said, "we saw and heard her talking through the machine to the people in the dwelling. This is what she said.

"'The wolf is part of our creation story, and therefore many Ojibwe have a strong spiritual connection to the wolf. Many Ojibwe believe the fate of the wolf is closely tied to the fate of all the Ojibwe. For these reasons the tribe feels the hunting and trapping of wolves is inappropriate.'"

"So these Ojibwe remember they are still Ojibwe," I said. "And they haven't forgotten the relationship they have with us, with wolves. They have said they will not allow the hunting of wolves on their lands. Having said that, however, the new humans will still be able to hunt on lands they control, even those lands within Ojibwe territory. While we might take some comfort in the Ojibwe decision, still, much of the land within

Ojibwe country is under the control of the new humans, so it will be very dangerous for us to venture out. The circle of our hunts takes us in and out of the lands of the Ojibwe and new humans.

"We need to hunt in order to live. We cannot hide in the deep of the bush.

"When you asked Auntie Ona and me several months back," I said to them that night when we gathered to talk story, "if the Ojibwe hunt wolves. No, they don't. Sometimes the things they do aren't ignorant. Sometimes they do things that remind us they are still Ojibwe."

—

That fall we continued to hunt, and with the addition of the young wolves we had more success. We wolves do not grow fat from the hunts. We remain lean. The young wolf that had often used the word 'stupid' had grown into the intelligent, strong hunter we knew he would become. He would be among the best warriors, we thought. As a new hunter he gave himself a humorous nickname *Bagwanagazi,* one who is dumb, in honor of the word he had so often used as a pup.

"My warrior name," he laughed. We wolves have that humor like our Ojibwe relatives. We're not afraid of making fun of ourselves.

He even teased the watchers whenever they would come among us, that maybe they enjoyed watching the machines the humans stare at a bit too much. And as he did we imagined the sight of a wolf staring through the opening in the human's dwelling, fixated at what it saw on the machine.

"I bet you enjoy it most when it shows dogs, or that place called Alaska because we heard moose are bigger there."

Even though the watchers have never been known for their humor they seemed to enjoy the teasing.

Anyway, we had been tracking several deer through the swamp up-river in *Nagachiwanong,* bottom of the lake (Fond du Lac Reservation in northern Minnesota). This is a beautiful place during any season, but especially so in the moon of falling leaves, when ice begins to form on the edges of the streams and bog lakes. I remember the day was clear and cold. Most of the leaves had fallen. We could see our breath as we ran along, getting closer to our prey.

Then I heard a sound, like the cracking of ice on the river in winter. I'd heard it before, many times, during the humans' hunting seasons, but always far off in the distance. Now it seemed the sound came from just alongside us.

I saw him fall.

My nephew died that day, my sister's son. Our collective fear quickly drove the rest of us away from the place that it happened. We ran for miles. And we didn't return to that place until late in the evening to find they had taken his body.

Our mournful calls went on for days and late into the evenings. Only after my mourning could I imagine his final words before he began his spirit journey.

"This is stupid," he would have said. Only then can I find solace from the senselessness of his death.

Sometimes when I cannot sleep and am up late into the evening, I look up in the sky at all the wonder there, at the path of stars that lead to the land of souls. And on those cold, fall evenings, all of our relatives who have walked on will sometimes appear there in the forever sky, dancing, dancing. And he will be there as well among all the warriors, hunters, teasing everyone near him about how funny they look when they try to dance as he moves so gracefully among them.

Bagwanagazi.

In the confusing times of the Sixth Fire, it is said that a group of visionaries came among the *Anishinabe*. They gathered all the priests of the *Midewiwin* (the spiritual teachings) Lodge. They told the priests that the *Midewiwin* Way was in danger of being destroyed. They gathered all of the sacred bundles. They gathered all the *Wee'gwas* (birch bark) scrolls that recorded the ceremonies. All these things were placed in a hollowed-out log from *Ma-none'* (the ironwood tree). Men were lowered over a cliff by long ropes. They dug a hole in the cliff and buried the log where no one could find it. Thus the teachings of the elders were hidden out of sight but not out of memory. It was said that when the time came that Indian people could practice their religion without fear that a little boy would dream where the ironwood log full of the sacred bundles and scrolls was buried. He would lead his people to the place.

—Benton-Banai, E. (1988). *The Mishomis Book*.
Hayward, WI: Indian Country Communications.

CHAPTER THIRTEEN

Little Boy

(Wisdom, Respect, Honesty, Truth, Love)

LOSING THEIR BROTHER AFFECTED THE young wolves and me as well. For them, I think it brought the realization that life is finite, that things can happen suddenly and without warning that change their world forever. That what happened to *Bagwanagazi* could have happened to any of them. That sometimes fate is the determinant of who lives, who dies. *Bagwanagazi* had been our trickster, funny, entertaining, talkative, opinionated, strong, handsome, and confident. He wasn't supposed to die but he did, and acknowledging it among the young wolves somehow hardened them, made them quieter, caused them to become more mature. Maybe it put into perspective the stories I had been telling them, that the lives of wolves are often harsh. And while that is certainly true, we also experience to its fullest all the goodness, the joy, that comes from life. We put all our physical, emotional, and spiritual energy into being wolves, the hunts, the posturing and competition for position within the pack, the way we care for our young and elderly and each other, the allegiance we show for the group over any individual. For our time here on *aki* is short, for most only several winters. I who have lived many winters have been the most fortunate among the pack.

I think losing yet another of the young among us brought into perspective my own fate, and to question why it was I had lived so long to witness the lives and passing of so many. And I suppose it made me realize as well that as story keeper I needed to assure the passing of all the stories from me to the young, not just the ones about humans I had been sharing with the lot of them.

There are stories that are reserved for a selected few, for I am also the keeper of the secret stories. And I knew it was time to make decisions about which of the young wolves I must choose to share those with as well. In life, *Bagwanagazi*, Youngest Nephew, and my little niece had been among my favorites. Now the decision was simple. One female, one male, the way it had been done for millennia. Two of each generation in each pack, to ensure the best we could that the stories, the secret ones, passed on down forever.

I noticed the young wolves seemed to linger around me more often now, particularly Youngest Nephew and niece, almost shadowing me. Maybe they knew somehow, intuitively, it was them whom I had chosen. I still teased them, even as we all went through the short period of mourning we wolves do. I try to use my humor every day. It's part of my nature.

"My niece," I began, "it seems your shadow has replaced mine. Could you tell yours to give mine some distance? He says he's missing being by me."

"Sorry, so sorry Uncle," she said, stepping back a bit but then just as quickly moving in close to me, burying her snout deep into my fur. She stayed there for the longest time, still, quiet.

"I am teasing you," I said. My niece. And although I didn't speak it aloud, the only thought that came to mind was that I loved her, as with all the young wolves, as though they were my own.

"I know, Uncle," she whispered back. Still, she remained burrowed deep into my shoulder.

"It's going to be okay," I reminded her. "Let him go. It's important you do that. Now, let him go."

Several days later she would come to me and thank me for reminding her of that. We wolves don't hang onto our grief. We allow the spirit of the one we lost to make that journey. Then we move on with our lives. That is what wolves do.

My nephew was the same. He went about it his own way.

"Nephew," I said, "could you turn your head the other way when you are up so close to me? Your breath, sometimes…."

"I think it was that old deer we ate the other day," he said. "It made me *boogat*, fart like mad."

"*Bagwanagazi* was master of the *boogat*," he continued. "Mine are nothing compared to his."

"I miss him as well," I said to my nephew.

"But I certainly don't miss his farts."

I think I mentioned it before but it's worth a reminder. Wolves use humor, the same as the Ojibwe, that survival humor; it is a medicine for bringing balance back into our lives.

—

"Tonight we're going to talk story," I began the night I called Youngest Nephew and niece together.

"But what of the rest?" asked Youngest Nephew.

"Just the two of you for the next several evenings," I replied. "Now, come for a walk with me."

We walked down the old trail that followed the hills above the river that flowed through *Nagachiwanong*, the bottom of the lake, all the way to the meadow where once had stood the village where the Ojibwe lived. Past the old stone foundations, rusted kettles, discarded cans, and broken bottles of the humans that had once lived there, just uphill from the place where humans and wolves, and all manner of animals, had once gone to escape the great fire. We moved so quietly that if a human had happened along the way while we were there they wouldn't even have noticed our presence. We are wolves.

Most all the leaves were gone as winter would soon be upon us, maybe just in days, and the sky was clear and filled with stars, the path of souls and the different spirits that live in the sky. We moved into the center of the meadow, marked by a large tree I had chosen as the place we would talk.

"Sit," I said.

"Ears in front, tails behind," I was teasing, of course, the same I had done when they were just little pups. Even in the times that are intended to be serious I sometimes insert that humor.

I told them then.

How many generations ago, when Ojibwe spiritual leaders saw how their people were suffering, when their spiritual ways were under attack and outlawed, and forced to become the practice of hidden ceremonies deep in the bush. They took their sacred teachings, I told the two young wolves, the bundles, scrolls of the ways of ceremony, and they put them in a log and buried it all into the side of a cliff somewhere along the shores of the big lake, the one that bears the likeness of a wolf. I said, someday, we don't know when, a little boy is going to find them, and bring them back among the people. And I said, when that day comes that will mark a new beginning for the Ojibwe, and for us as well, because humans and wolves, we're the same.

The same.

"That's not all though," I continued on with the story to the two young wolves. "That part of the story I just told you is common knowledge among the Ojibwe, at least the ones who know the importance of remembering and telling their stories. That story is scratched on the paper they make from the meat of trees, and has been preserved on the machines they stare at all the time. What I want to share with you is something else.

"Wolves know the hiding place. And I will take the two of you there so you know it as well.

"For the story had been told to my sister, the one who had died trying to protect her pups, and to me, by Old Uncle, and to him and his sister by his auntie, going back in time for many, many generations, because back when the bundles and scrolls were buried, our watchers were there, hidden in and among the trees, bush, hidden only as we do so well, wolves."

—

Several days later I went to *Ginew,* Golden Eagle, the beta male, and *Ogema,* Leader. First to *Ginew* as was our practice.

"I need to take Youngest Nephew and niece away for several days, on a journey, to show them something and talk story," I said to *Ginew.*

"And we need the three of you here to hunt, " he replied. I knew that. We need to hunt continuously in order to survive.

"I know," I said, "but this is important.

"This is something they need to see, to hear. This cannot wait any longer. Once the snows begin we might have to delay until spring. Maybe it will be too late by then. I'm old, you know. I could get stuck in the snow this winter and not be able to get out." I continued, even faking a limp as I spoke. Sometimes I even use that humor on the adults.

Ginew was begrudging, like he was most of the time. That's his job. Yet even he knew the importance of talking story, of passing it down through the generations. He took me to *Ogema.*

"Tell them everything," his reply. He never did use a lot of words.

We set out early the next morning heading east, following the trails that ran parallel to the river toward the big lake. Along the way we had to skirt several of the new humans' settlements, cross many roads, fields, but stayed mostly deep in the bush. By the end of the first day we came to the sacred mountain of the Ojibwe, where below lay the island of spirits where the Ojibwe had once gathered. There I reminded the two of the time just several months earlier when I had taken them to that place.

"Remember, *Zhi-shay',*" said Youngest Nephew, "I thought I needed to seek a vision like the male humans in order to find my purpose, my reason for being? I think back sometimes to when I was a little pup and how I thought and said some pretty foolish things. Like about dogs. I know

now that I have no reason to hate all dogs, after hearing the story of Bear and *Ma'iingan*."

"Have you thought at all about what your role might be within the pack when you are old enough?" I asked. I wanted him to be thinking about it. Sometimes we wolves give our advice in the form of questions. Most of the time, however, we do so by talking story. The lessons, advice, are hidden in the stories. Advice giving is sideways that way, never straight on, the same as our Ojibwe relatives.

"I think someday I could be alpha male," he replied. "But sometimes I'm not sure. Sometimes I think maybe that wouldn't be enough. Do you know what I mean, Uncle? I'm just unsure of what that other role might be. I know now that I will also be the story keeper."

"I understand," I replied, " I think you could be leader if that is your decision. Remember the story I told about your Uncle *Zhigag*, Skunk, who found himself in the position of being the omega. I'm sure that when he was a pup he would never have even dreamed of being the omega. Who would have that dream? I think sometimes that life, circumstances, fate, we don't know what, the Creator, these other things decide for us. And your brother who was killed with the stick that breathes fire. I'm sure he didn't know when he was a little pup that his life would end so early, the way it did.

"I think we make conscious and unconscious decisions about the direction of our lives, Nephew. We make decisions, set a goal, and then life also has its way with us.

"And what about you, my niece?" I looked her way.

"I'm pretty sure what I want to be," she replied. "I think I'm a good hunter. I been learning them lessons from my mother and aunties, and of course you. I know as well that I want to be the story keeper, like you, Uncle. The stories, when I hear them, they come alive in my head. I think maybe that's what I'll be, a good hunter, the storyteller."

There was purpose in what I was doing with them, talking story as we went along. And as we waited for darkness, when we would skirt the new humans' city of *Onigamising* (Duluth) and sister city across the bay, *Odana* town (Superior), we talked some more.

So with darkness we swam across the river just south of the new human settlements and began making our way along the rim of the big lake, crossing more fields, trying not to awaken dogs.

"We'll hunt tomorrow," I told them. "I'm getting hungry, aren't you?"

"I could eat a horse," laughed my niece, kiddingly.

"Sister, it might take a whole woods full of us to bring one of them down," laughed her brother.

So the next day we took some time to find sustenance, and at the end of the day we were able to harvest a young deer. As elder adult, I got to eat the contents of the body cavity, a delicacy, something I hadn't done since the days I was the alpha. My face, covered in blood, I nearly ate myself sick.

We buried some, of course, a cache, that we would retrieve on our way back home.

We slept well that night, but before we did I talked story with them about the forever sky, and told them again the stories about the spirits that live in the sky at that time between fall and winter.

"Are there wolves out there, Uncle?" they both asked as we lay there, looking skyward. "I mean alive ones, not just spirit ones."

"Of course there are," I reminded them. "Remember the story of *Ma'iingan Mikan*, the wolf's trail, the one my brother told me?"

"You've told us so many stories," they said. "Sometimes it's hard to remember them all."

"You need to listen harder," I scolded them. "Remember that. That's very important. You need to listen not just with your head, but your whole body, your spirit as well. I'm not going to be here forever. It's going to be your turn someday, who knows when, maybe soon."

"Besides, neither of you are smart enough to create new stories." I was teasing them, of course.

We slept then.

Just before dawn we set out again, heading east along the big lake, crossing several rivers, up and down the ridges that border the lake. Off in the distance one of the new humans' trails, the sound of the machines they rode in. We trotted along mostly in silence, now making only occasional conversation.

"There are wolves along our journey and there will be a another pack of our relatives east of where the Ojibwe hid the teachings," I told them. "In a place the new humans call Echo Valley, and what the Ojibwe know as *Miskwabekong*, the place of the red cliffs. The wolves will leave us be, they won't bother us. The place I am taking you is sacred to both wolves and humans, one of the most sacred of places. The wolves along the way of our journey and those of *Miskwabekong* will know why we are here."

We made our way well into the evening that day, and then I told them we were there. "Rest now," I told them. "Tomorrow."

That night we all lay there, maybe a bit apprehensive about what tomorrow would reveal to them. I hadn't been there since I was a young wolf myself, then with my sister and Old Uncle.

The dancers came out that night as we lay there, just before the young wolves and I went to asleep. They covered the whole of the northern sky. The spirits the new humans call the northern lights, my mother and father, Old Uncle, my sister and brother, and of course *Bagwanagazi*.

We stood then. Threw our heads back.

And sang for them.

—

We were awoken the next morning by the snap of a twig coming from somewhere close nearby.

"*Bizaan*," I said to the young wolves. Quiet.

Rising quickly, we walked through some cedar and fern and then, while hiding behind a large yellow birch, saw him.

"The little boy," both the young wolves whispered to me at the same time. He was a young Ojibwe boy, maybe seven or eight winters.

"*Bizaan,*" I said again, barely whispering.

We followed him then as he made his way toward the lake, which could be seen off in the distance, quietly, as wolves do. The closer we got to the lake, the deeper the ridges and hollows, another stream to cross, boulders bigger than the new humans' machines that carried them this way and that.

Then we came to the lake, to the red cliffs, the sound of the waves as they pounded away, the blue of sky and deep blue-green of the waters below.

"Watch now," I said to the young wolves.

And we watched as the little boy retrieved rope from the pack he was wearing, securing one end to a cedar tree that grew from the rocky outcropping. Then he tied the other end of the rope firmly around his waist, and began to lower himself down over the side of the cliff.

To a cave that was halfway down, and when he got there he climbed in. It seemed he was in there the longest time. I didn't have to even tell the young wolves we would have waited forever, if we had to, until he came out.

But soon enough he did, and in his pack were the bundles, the scrolls.

My heart was singing an old, old song shared only between wolves and our Ojibwe relatives. My niece and nephew, myself, wolves so overcome with joy we wept, silently, so powerful that moment.

Then the little boy began pulling himself up to the top of the cliff. He stood there for a moment dusting his self off. Then he looked our way, smiling.

And disappeared before our very eyes.

Now in the winter of my time on this earth, memory often takes me down the old road that overlooks the river that flows through *Nagachi-wanong* (the bottom of the lake, Fond du Lac Reservation in northern Minnesota). It seems the whole story of my life sings in chorus along the way of that journey, in all its various cadences, octaves and ranges, and moods, and in my childhood voice and that of an adult. Along the way I recognize all the sounds and smells and bright colors, and the many angles of sunlight though the trees in their seasons. And I know the dark road equally as well. This place, this road walked with parents and uncles and aunties, brothers and sisters and cousins, nephews and nieces. This place walked alone. This place journeyed. This place run upon, laughed upon, danced upon, wept upon – this life of great joy and great sorrow.

The spirits of the living inform the bright sky and soothing rain and wind and waving summer flowers of this place. Bittersweet memories of loved ones who have passed on inform the moonless nights, sunless winters, and heavy air. For my life has been all of these things and more, in a continuous play of light and shadow, a dance of hope and despair.

My life. My life.

CHAPTER FOURTEEN

Youngest Nephew, Little Niece

(Wisdom, Respect, Truth, Love)

Zhi-shay'

WE TALKED ABOUT THE LITTLE boy all the way home.

"*Zhi-shay'*," they asked, "What about this? What about that?"

And with each succeeding set of pups, it seemed I always faced similar questions. So I would respond in this way:

"Wolves are the shadow dance partners of humans. The pair cannot exist without the other. We are the same and opposite, yin and yang, shadow and light. Ours is an intricate relationship."

Then I would talk story.

I did this until I ran out of words.

—

The Creator said that to forever remember the close kinship of wolf and human, whatever happened to one would befall the other, for both there would be times of great happiness and great sadness, of hope and despair. That is the way of things. And the Creator said these things that would one day become true: One day, the Creator said, each of you will be hunted to near extinction. Each of you will lose your lands. But those difficult times will not go on forever, the Creator said.

"Someday you will live out my beautiful dream for you."

I can't presume to know the Creator's dream, of course, but I have my imaginings. I wish wolves would be allowed to be wolves, to live as we once did. I wish we were not hunted or caged or put in pens to be observed, or trapped or have our pelts sold and made into things. I wish the new humans would fully accept their shared responsibility with the Ojibwe and other tribes to care for this beautiful garden that is *aki*.

And what of the Ojibwe, what do I wish for them? I wish the Ojibwe would remain Ojibwe, and always remember that they share a parallel existence with their brothers and sisters, wolves. I wish they would live according to *mino-bimaadiziwin*, the Good Path, that assures all life is honored, where kindness is considered the highest of virtues. That they would share food and other necessities as they once did, that they have a strong group identity. These ways are very different from the values of individualism, competitiveness, and materialism too many of them live by today, where their communities have inequalities of rich or poor, employed and unemployed, haves and have nots. That they would return to their old ways of caring for orphans and children who cannot live with their parents, where there is no need for an "Indian" Child Welfare Act. Where women and men are equal. Where men do not abandon their families or abuse their partners. Where elders are revered. Where crime is rare, and when it is committed it is harshly dealt with. Where there are no gangs, drugs, or alcohol.

I wish they would return to governing themselves using their clan system, when temporary shared leadership was egalitarian and based on moral leadership, where important decisions were made using consensus and involved the whole community. When leadership was something not sought, when good leaders stepped back and let others speak first. When leaders spoke only when they had something important to say.

I guess that's a big to do list. Maybe after I walk on and have been in the land of souls for a while and feel more comfortable with the place, I'll ask for a sit down with the Creator and share it.

Little Niece

When *Zhi-shay'* was too old to hunt, I would insist to the others that I be the one to bring him something to eat. For the time soon came when it was I who led the hunts. If he were sleeping, as he so often was, I would nudge him just a bit upon my return.

"Uncle?" I would say to awaken him, and he would slowly open his eyes, groggily saying something about me being his favorite little niece, even knowing that I was no longer a pup, nor little, nor a young wolf. I lead now, the females. It happened quickly and easily for me. My mother, father, uncle and aunties, they taught me well.

I knew as well that I would be the storyteller when I was Old Auntie. And someday I would lead several pups that I had chosen for their journey east to the place along the big lake, the one that bore the likeness to a wolf, to the red cliffs, the cave, and the little boy. The circle continued that way.

I regurgitated my food for him. Uncle, his teeth now soft, eyes tired.

I did this for some time and then one day when I returned from hunt to camp he was no longer there.

"Uncle?" I said to the wind, air.

———

Over the past several seasons with each litter of pups I have talked story to them about my uncle, the things he taught me, values he reinforced in the way he lived his life. I try to do the same myself, live those values. I do it naturally. And I speak highly to them about our relatives, the Ojibwe. I want wolves to know about them in a good way. This is what I say.

Generosity is love being acted upon, and we, wolves and humans, have always been generous. In cultures that were built around the needs of the group rather than individuals, sharing is reinforced on a daily basis so it became deeply ingrained in our thinking and culture. Our ancestors would not have survived without it. When the new humans came among Ojibwe people they noticed and made note of their generosity. They would typically be gifted with whatever it was when one of the new humans would remark how much they liked something of the Ojibwe.

I taught each group of pups that despite the adoption of the new humans' values such as materialism and individualism among many Ojibwe people, the value of generosity remains strong in their communities. At the summer powwows there will always be a group of youth and adults bringing food plates to elders and the disabled at feast time. And when their families suffer the loss of a loved one, food and this paper they call money, which they exchange for things, will appear at their doors from all over their community, from the programs the workers in their government have designed to serve the humans, from friends and neighbors, many of whom are poor and who have little else to give. Some will come just to sit and visit, and give the gift of friendship and understanding. For they along with everyone else in their communities have experienced many difficult periods of grieving as well, sharing the two attributes necessary for empathy – the experience of knowing what others are going through as well as feeling their pain, the affect. They will bring tobacco and their dwellings will be filled with blue smoke, muffled voices and laughter. Because even in mourning Ojibwe people find reason for laughter in the stories they are sharing. Even the stories are a gift.

And among the Ojibwe someone will always bring firewood and they and others will take turns tending the outside mourning fire that is kept burning for four days until the spirit of their loved one has reached the land of souls. Humans who barely know the family, who have nothing, will come to their doors and offer their condolences. And when it is time to sing, a group of them will join together around the drum, and their voices will go deep into their hearts and take them back in time to when the Ojibwe were strong and powerful, and their singing will blend with the laughter of their young, cousins and little brothers and sisters playing in the bedrooms, the smells of strong coffee, lugalate, made from the grains of wheat, and wild rice hot dish, and pan after pan of casseroles. All of this will mingle and become one and carry outside and become part of the wood smoke rising from the mourning fire up into the cold air and sky filled with thousands upon thousands of stars, each one representing the souls of our ancestors. And just at that moment in their darkest time they will be whole again, strong and powerful.

And all during this time, we wolves will be listening from deep in the bush. We are the same, I say to the pups, the same.

—

I tell the pups that I try to live those values and they should as well, the ones brought down from the sky world by the little boy. It's hard, I know. I have failed many times myself. Wolves and humans are imperfect be-ings. We all stray from the trail, become lost sometimes. And even know-ing there are many Ojibwe who have forgotten the values, what it truly means to be Ojibwe, there are an equal number or more of them who still try to live them as well. I try to keep it simple at first, the teachings. When they get older and we gather to talk story I will fill in the details – wisdom, respect, honesty, humility, truth, bravery, and love.

"Which is most important?" one of the pups will always ask.

"*Zagaa'idiwin*, love," I say.

Love is when you open your heart and let the Creator in, and let it live through you by the way you conduct yourself, the way you walk through life, for the Creator's love is all of the values combined and more.

I pray for them every night before I join the huddle of ears, tails, and fur. The Ojibwe. They are on my list, right after us, wolves. That we make it through all our struggles, that we never forget who we are.

Ojibwe.

Wolves.

—

When I became an adult I took on my big wolf name, *Waabishki-Ma'iingan Equay*, White Wolf Woman, a long name for sure, probably too long for most to pronounce, let alone remember. Uncle would always tease me about it.

"I nearly run out of breath whenever I try to talk your name," he would say.

"Is it okay if I just call you little *boogaf*?"

Youngest Nephew

I don't think I ever got the image of the little boy out of my head. He remained there, always in the back of my mind as I grew into adulthood and made decisions about what direction my life would take.

I suppose one day I could have become the alpha, to eventually succeed *Ogema*, Leader. However, I would have had to be patient. *Ogema* was a good leader, strong, rare with words, always treating the pack respectfully, making decisions for the good of the group. And although *Giniw*, Golden Eagle, the beta male, was a loyal enforcer of the alpha, I never felt he had what it took to be alpha.

Even as a young adult I knew that if I wanted to I could take him, make him submit. Some might think the way we do these things is harsh, but it's the way of wolves. In the end, however, I would leave that to another in the pack. My heart just wasn't in it.

I told Uncle of my decision once it was made, sister as well. My desire was to become a watcher, to return to that place east along the big lake where I had seen the little boy retrieve the bundles, the scrolls. My intention would be to live as a lone wolf until there was an opening in the Echo Valley pack, the ones known by the Ojibwe as the wolves of *Miskwabekong*, the wolves from the place of the red cliffs.

"I'll never see you again, Youngest Nephew," said Uncle.

And when he said that I lifted my snout skyward and replied, "I'll see you up there."

Our watchers had noticed for generations that the Ojibwe often point with their lips.

"Pass those potatoes," they'll say when sitting around their dinner tables. Then they'll point with their lips toward the potatoes.

"Pass me that fry bread," and they'll point with their lips again off in the direction of the fry bread.

Well, I don't know if anyone has ever noticed, but wolves, we really don't have what you could call lips. So when we set out to copy the Ojibwe, to point the way they do, we use our snouts instead.

"Pass that rabbit head this way," we say, pointing with our snout.

"Pass that deer leg this way," we say, again pointing with our snout.

I got that teasing humor from Uncle, I think.

Anyway, when I made the decision to go east to *Miskwabekong*, I didn't know if I would ever see my sister again either, at least not in this life, but she reminded me.

"I'll see you again someday," she told me, "when I travel that way with pups to show them that sacred place, the little boy."

"And don't try to keep us away from there either," she teased.

"I'll kick your butt."

So I set out on that journey, and when I reached the place where we had witnessed the little boy, I set up camp somewhere above the ridgeline in the hills that ring the big lake. I waited, listening to the calls of the wolves of Echo Valley, and waited some more. And then one day, some months later, I noticed in their calls they were missing a warrior voice. An opening. I returned the call then, and then went among them, submissive, as is our tradition, culture, and was accepted as a member of the pack. With time, I moved up in the hierarchy that is wolves to beta male, then alpha. I remained in that position for several years.

When it was time to turn the pack over to a younger male I did so without a struggle. I walked away from the fight, not out of any loss of dignity or lack of courage. I knew my next role was in being a watcher.

So that is what I do.

I spend most of my days and many evenings now just on the outskirts of the village of Ojibwe humans that is *Miskwabekong*, the place of the red cliffs. In the bush, hidden, silent, a watcher. We need to know, us wolves, that there are still Ojibwe, that there are still those among them who live those values, who remember the story of First Human and *Ma'iingan* Wolf, and the naming of *aki*.

They seem to continue to have their struggles. All the pieces, the things that fall away when their culture is no longer strong enough to hold them together as a people are still there, the poverty of spirit, alcohol and drugs, gangs and on and on. I see, however, a growing awareness with them, especially among the young. They seem to realize that the Ojibwe will not have the ability to put back together all the shattered parts of their being without the ultimate freedom to imagine their future and make it real. Their government talks of self-determination, but real self-determination, at least from the perspective of wolves, is imagining the future and making it real. Only then will they remain Ojibwe.

We know because we make our own decisions about our future.

We still live. We remain wolves.

What I am talking about is freeing the mind and the imagination, asking themselves what is it about being Ojibwe that they will bring into the future. The question itself goes far beyond any kind of economic, social, or political solutions they seek. The issue is about them, and what they have become.

And it is obvious the Ojibwe are inherently much more complicated and diverse a people than their ancestors. They have many more individual choices regarding their multiple identities, including their Ojibwe identities, than their ancestors. And maybe this is a good thing. All humans, regardless of their cultural identity, should be free to make choices that make them feel whole, give them hope, and allow them to dream their own future and make it real. At the same time they will need to collectively make decisions as a tribe, before time and the lure of all that is the new humans' culture decides for them. Before what is being taught to their young in schools and on the machines they stare at decides. Before all of the forces within the human world that insist everyone be the same decide for them.

——

My Uncle always said I was a bit preachy. Sorry about that.

So, anyway, one day I was watching from the edge of a field at their powwow grounds. They like their powwows. I was getting really hungry from the smells coming from their cook tents. We wolves have these really sensitive noses, no way that's going to change. Fry bread this and fry bread that, wild rice hot dish, corn soup, buffalo burgers. I'm getting hungrier just thinking about it.

They have these traditions they follow when they do the powwows, even knowing these are social occasions someone made up not too many seasons ago to entertain the tourists. Let's show the tourists who we are, one of them must have said. We'll pound on drums and put on our outfits and sing really, really loud, and we'll dance, and maybe they'll understand us better, us Ojibwe. Maybe they'll even treat us better, more as equals, instead of like *moo*, poop.

I'm not sure of any wisdom in that decision. It's not for me to judge.

Anyway, there I was, lying in the weeds, the bush, as they did their grand entry, when all the dancers come into the circle of the arena to an honor song. Their warriors always lead the dance, carrying eagle feather staffs and various flags, things made from the meat of certain plants that represent the different tribal and new humans' nations, packs. The male dancers of various sorts enter next, what they call their traditional dancers, grass dancers, then the male fancy dancers. The females enter next, women's traditional dancers, then the jingle dress dancers. The jingles are made from a shiny metal and when they touch they make a sound when they dance. At one time they were made with the lids of snuff cans, filled with a plant that was chewed, but nowadays there are not enough snuff chewers so they make them lids just for jingles. Then the women's fancy shawl dancers enter, followed by the boys, then the little girls.

I saw him when the little boys entered the dance area. He was with his mother or an auntie, who was holding his hand as he toddled about, trying his best to dance, to step in beat with the drum. Everyone in the audience that rings the dance area was standing, some clapping, smiling, most all looking proud, drummers singing just high. Then some of the female dancers encircled the drummers and began singing as well.

The whole story of humans and wolves flashed in my mind as I began to sing as well, an old, old song shared only between wolves and humans.

Maybe he was three, four winters old. I would have recognized him anywhere, even knowing when I first saw him that one and only time before he was maybe seven or eight winters old when *Zhi-shay'* and sister and I were at that sacred place where the bundles, the scrolls were hidden.

The little boy.

BIBLIOGRAPHY

Benton-Banai, E. (1988). The Mishomis Book. Hayward, WI: Indian Country Communications.

"Island History," Madeline Island Chamber of Commerce, *madeli-neisland.com/madeline-island/island-history* (accessed Nov. 21, 2019).

Johnston, B. (1976). Ojibway Heritage. Lincoln, NE: University of Nebraska Press.

Peacock, T. Ed. (1998). A Forever Story: The People and Community of the Fond du Lac Reservation. Cloquet, MN: Fond du Lac Band of Lake Superior.

Peacock, T. and Wisuri, M. (2002). The Good Path. Afton, MN: Afton Historical Society Press.

Peacock, T. and Wisuri, M. (2002). Ojibwe *Waasa Inaabidaa* We Look in All Directions. Afton, MN: Afton Historical Society Press.

Peacock, T. (2019). The Forever Sky. St. Paul, MN: Minnesota Historical Society Press.

Wikipedia contributors, "List of gray wolf populations by country," *Wikipedia, The Free Encyclopedia, en.wikipedia.org/w/index.php?title=List_of_gray_wolf_populations_by_country&oldid=926336697* (accessed November 24, 2019).

ABOUT THE AUTHOR

Thomas D. Peacock has authored or co-authored *The Forever Story, Collected Wisdom, Ojibwe Waasa Inaabidaa: We Look in All Directions, The Good Path, The Seventh Generation, The Four Hills of Life, To Be Free, The Tao of Nookomis, Beginnings: The Homeward Journey of Donovan Manypenny, The Forever Sky,* and *The Dancers. Ojibwe* and *The Good Path* were Minnesota Book Award winners. *The Seventh Generation* was multicultural children's book of the year (American Association of Multicultural Education). He is a member of the Fond du Lac Band of Lake Superior Anishinaabe Ojibwe and lives with his wife Betsy in Little Sand Bay, Red Cliff, Wisconsin and Duluth, Minnesota. For more information about wolves, the Ojibwe, and the relationship of wolves and the Ojibwe, please visit *www.thewolfstrail.com*

ABOUT THE COVER ARTIST

James O'Connell lives and paints in Madison, Wisconsin. He continues to draw inspiration from the years he lived in California and the desert southwest, as well as his native Twin Cities. Early retirement enabled him to explore new artistic subjects and styles. Over 500 of his original paintings and prints now are hung in homes and businesses across the country. Publishers have also found his images colorful, imaginative and fanciful – enhancing their book covers and periodicals.

2-james-oconnell.pixels.com (Fine Art America)